Beneath a Big Sky
Stories and Poems

The BigSky Writers

The stories and poems contained in this collection are works of fiction. Names, characters, places and events portrayed are either products of the author's imagination or are used fictitiously. Any character resemblance to actual persons living or dead is entirely co-incidental.

Copyright © 2014 BigSky Writers

All rights reserved.

All rights reserved. No part of this work may be reproduced or transmitted in any form or by any means, electronic or mechanical without written permission from the authors.

ISBN: 150323116X
ISBN-13: 978-1503231160

DEDICATION

To Rosemarie

'We all had the enjoyment and the privilege of working with Rosemarie for a while. She always had a brisk, accurate, interested and often humorous, word or two to offer in discussion, and many rich and lively words ready for any 'exercise' set for us, some of which are included here.

Thank you, Rosemarie. We are glad we knew you. You remain in our thoughts.'

To Nikki

'Nikki shoots a straight arrow. She knows what's what (so important for a Tutor!) and says it. She also cares a great deal about everyone's efforts, and about their finer feelings, and respects points of view (even more important in a Creative Writing Tutor!) But she also spends time beyond the call of duty, gently teasing apart the very roots of our writing and helping us to replant them the correct distance apart and in the right order (maybe that's the ultimate?).

Well, we think she's really good and deserves the George Cross or its equivalent.

Thanks, Nikki!'

CONTENTS

A Gleam on Orion's Belt
    By Nicola McDonagh   1
The Door
    By Mike Moody   7
Holiday Let
    By Joan Roberts   11
Mistaken Identity
    By Joan Roberts   12
Owen
    By Will Ingrams   16
The Ship of Fools
    By Rosemarie Czarnocka   23
Tell Me The Truth
    By Judith Osborne   26
Revenge
    By Anne F. Clarke   27
Survival
    By D. Green   28
Tony and Cleo
    By Joan Roberts   32
'A Page Torn out of Time and Space'
    By Judith Osborne   35
Arrivals Hall, Pearly Gates
    By John Antram   40
Do You Believe in Love at First Sight?
    By Joan Roberts   41
Doctor Undressing
    By John Antram   46
The Male Swan
    By Joan Roberts   49
Copy, Copier, Copiest
    By John Antram   53
Time
    By D. Green   55
Rainy Day
    By Will Ingrams   56
Framgnam Wannabe Man's Lucky Day
    By Mike Moody   62
Four Years of Adversity
    By Rosemarie Czarnocka   66

The Monkey Pipe	
By Will Ingrams	70
Round The Bend	
By Mike Moody	73
Fire	
By D. Green	85
The Tabby Cat	
By Anne F. Clarke	87
Domestic Beasts	
By Will Ingrams	88
Perfect	
By D. Green	89
Arachnophobia	
By Rosemarie Czarnocka	95
A Very Special Cat	
By Anne F. Clarke	99
Complement of the Shooting Season	
By John Antram	107
Fenland Incident	
By Judith Osborne	108
Give the Dog a Bonus	
By John Antram	112
A Thief?	
By Judith Osborne	113
Felicity's Fall	
By Will Ingrams	122
Diptych, On and off the Wall	
By Judith Osborne	132
The Teapot	
By Anne F. Clarke	135
The Musings of Herbert Prew	
By D. Green	139
Secateurs and Saboteurs	
By John Antram	145
Who Do You Think You Are?	
By Joan Roberts	147
The Colonel and the Fly	
By Joan Roberts	149
The Yew Tree	
By Anne F. Clarke	152
The Annual Garden Party	
By Joan Roberts	157

A GLEAM ON ORION'S BELT

Nicola McDonagh

The young woman with the gold nose ring lay on her back amongst the dew tipped grass and counted the constellations. Some she knew by name, others not. She pointed at a swirling cluster of bright dots and said, 'The Laughing in Chaos nebula.' She heard him sigh, the fourth one in less than an hour. 'Isn't the sky beautiful?'
 'What?'
 'The sky.'
 'Eh?'
 'Look at the vastness, the bright dots of light that sparkle. Ryan, actually look up. Don't you see how beautiful it is?'
 'I see how beautiful you are,' Ryan said and stroked her leg. She flicked his hand away as though it were a gnat. Ryan leant back on his elbows and sighed a sigh so big that the leaves on the elderflower bush above his head, quivered. She screwed up her eyes for a moment and then sat up. A light breeze swished through the dense hedgerow and whispered of coming cloud and rain. She turned to Ryan, who rolled onto his belly. 'Ow! Bloody ants. I don't know how you can sit there with all these insects biting the crap out of you.'
 'They don't seem to bother me.'
 'Lucky you. I'm going in.'
 'No, wait, Ryan. Stay.'
 'What for?'
 The woman did not answer. She raised her gaze to the night sky and smiled. 'For this. What else?'
 'Amber, what is wrong with you?'
 'Nothing.'

The breeze became stronger bringing a tinge of autumn cold. Ryan shook as goose bumps popped up on his well-tanned flesh. Amber did not move. She sat still like a garden ornament and breathed in the change in seasons.

'Aren't you cold?'

'No.'

'I am.'

'Go inside then.'

'Come with me.'

'No. I'm watching.'

'For what?'

'For a shooting star.'

'Why?'

'Because that boy I was looking after in the ICU said they were souls searching for a new body.'

He laughed and she sat up.

'Paul had a journal. The doctors kept it with his files. I had a look one day. Amazing. The things he wrote in there were just so deep. I read some of it to him now and again. I swear that when I did, he knew. His eyelids would flutter and his mouth would twitch.' Amber hugged her knees and continued, 'I memorised some of it. "There is a special light that shines from stars. It does not burn or take your breath away like the rays from the sun. Starlight soothes. Starlight flickers in hidden code. There are some that can decipher it, and when they do, an agreement is made with the universe to keep the secret unsolved. To all but the chosen few."'

'Yeah, well, he was a nutter wasn't he?'

'Was he? Just because some so-called experts said so, doesn't mean that he was. No, he wasn't insane. Paul knew, he saw and heard things we can only dream about.'

'What about the things he did? You know, writing using his shit? Nah, he was a psycho. He was a dangerous schizophrenic.'

'He wasn't dangerous.'

'Amber, he jumped from a six story building onto a parked
car. I'd call that dangerous.'

Amber gulped and bit her lower lip. 'I believe he fell, not
jumped. I think he found out a truth that scientists and theologians have been searching for since mankind began to wonder where we came from and what it all means.'

Ryan snorted. 'He really got to you didn't he. You're too soft for this psychiatric nursing work.'

'Maybe, but I know I reached him.'

'Yeah, well, they do say that some people in a coma know what's going on around them.'

'Paul did. I know for sure.'

'How?'

'When they turned off the life support, he smiled. After they left me alone with him I opened the curtains to let the moon and the stars in. He opened his eyes for a split second and I swear I heard him laugh.'

'You imagined it, you saw what you wanted to see, heard what you wanted to hear.'

Amber looked at Ryan and tried not to let the tears fall, but they did. He leant forward and wiped them away with his fingertips. He stroked her cheek and said, 'Come on, Amber, let's go in before we catch a cold.'

Amber tilted her head towards the night sky. 'You go, Ryan. I want to feel the light from the stars. I want to know what Paul knew.'

'Look, all he knew was how to get under your skin, that's all. Why are you being so weird?'

'Am I?'

'Well, yeah. Come on, stop all this stupid stuff and let's go to bed.'

Ryan stood and held out his hand. Amber stared at his redundant fingers and Ryan let his arm flop against his thigh. A cold breeze swished around his ankles and he shivered. 'Are you coming?'

'No.'

Ryan turned and walked away. Amber took a breath of autumn air, closed her eyes and filled her lungs with microscopic life that she could not see, but felt die deep within her alveoli. A shooting star flashed across the glimmering heavens. Bright and swift it disappeared before her tight-closed lids could open. When they did, Amber saw an echo from its tail and heard the pulse of something far away.

The click of a key turning in a lock caused Amber to turn her head. Ryan glared at her from behind the kitchen window. He opened it and said, 'Since you like the great outdoors so much, you can stay out there all night.' He threw a pillow and a duvet out of the window and slammed it shut. Amber sniffed, stood up and ambled to where the bedclothes lay. She picked them up and held them against her chest and watched Ryan through the glass. He moved around the small white room like a robot. Mechanically he filled a glass with water and drank it down in one great gulp, then rinsed the tumbler. He did not look up to witness Amber glare at him. She moved towards the pane and breathed on it. Through the haze she made, Amber saw Ryan turn off the light switch. Now there was blackness on the inside as well as out.

Amber pulled the duvet around her shoulders and stepped away from the small house with the broken rendering and missing plaster. She strode across the large garden, pushed her way through the brambles and wandered out onto the newly harvested fields. With the light from the moon to guide her, Amber walked over the stubbled ground until she came to a small thicket of trees. She touched the orange-tinged leaves and smiled when they fell quietly onto the mulch beneath her feet.

Amber lay the pillow on the floor below a gnarled oak tree and spread the duvet out. She lay on her back and let her head rest amongst the twigs and moss. She felt a scratch at the back of her neck, moved her hand to the where it stung, and touched something cold and hard. She wrapped her fingers around the neck of a broken bottle and sat up. A warmth slid down her neck and arm, but Amber didn't notice. Her eyes were fixed on the jagged bottle that was tipped in red. She wiped the soil away from the glass, held it up to the faint glow of the moon and said, "The stars are winking at us. They know a secret we must have."

Amber saw the blood surround her body. From her high vantage point she could see it outline her shape like a viscous second skin. The red contrasted with the white shirt and trousers she wore and for moment Amber thought she was a giant strawberry floating in a sea of yoghurt.

Her vision faltered.

The white became black.

***

A thumping sound in her ears slowed and faded. An absolute quiet embraced Amber, cradling and swaying her until all was numbness. Her eyes became part of the night sky blinking with the stars, seeing infinity through a speck of light.

A hum, low and sonorous entered her veins. They pulsed in time to the ancient rhythm sending sparks of electrical currents crackling through her body. Sleeping neurons woke and breathed in the ether of the universe. Amber heard everything - the chatter of existence in all its varied forms speak of then and now and what will be. She understood why, and for the first time didn't care.

From within this din of origin, came a voice of recognition. 'I knew you understood.'

'Paul?'

'Yeah.'

'You were right.'

'I am. Lose the past tense, Nose ring.'

'Is that what you called me?'

'It was all I really saw of you. The sun caught the gold sometimes and flashed into my eyes. You were that lightning, that splash of bright that made my shaded world bearable. I knew I'd find you here.'

'Where are we?'

'Everywhere.'

'I see.'

'Good. So, take a look.'

Amber did and saw Ryan. Saw his grief in stop motion stutters like the beating of a moth wing. She tried to reach out to him, to soften the pain and brush away the sad that fell from his lashes. 'Nah, that's not the way you do it.'

'Then how?'

'The code. Use the pulse method. It's by far the most effective way to make the unready listen and take note.'

'I don't know how.'

'Hitch a ride on that comet. It's full of folk like you and me desperate to say goodbye, or hello, depending on your philosophy. He'll see that. When you get to earths atmosphere, begin the blinking. You do know Morse code, don't you?'

'No, and I guarantee, Ryan doesn't either.'

'If I could actually sigh, I would, in despair of so-called human advancement. What simpleton decided to get rid of mankind's only universal way to communicate? Look, flutter your baby blues and send him your message, he'll understand. Trust me.'

Amber felt a glow surround her. A huge ache pulled from within propelled her forward towards a shriek of light and noise and babbling. Her ears bombarded with cross conversations; voices talking all at once in languages she could not understand. A white wind ripped at her face, or where her face used to be, and Amber called to Paul, 'You're fading. I can't feel you.'

'Ah. Not yet. You're not ready.'

'I am.'

'No. Go back. He's pulling you, not me.'

'It's strong, his yearning.'

'As strong as yours.'

'Do I have to say goodbye to you?'

'Nah. Look to the sky sometime and I'll be there. You'll recognise the twitch.'

***

Amber felt a pain.

And another.

A sharp, stabbing agony that clutched with vicious fingers at her chest and dug fingernails right into her heart. She could not breath.

'Shocking.'

Amber sucked in air.

'Okay, she's with us now.'

Amber saw a face.

Ryan smiled at her. She looked over his beaming countenance and up into the blue-black sky. Amongst the millions of flashing stars, one shone brighter than the others. It winked at her and she blinked back.

'You're a lucky girl, you know.'

'I know, Ryan.'

'I saw the shooting star. It passed over here,' Ryan said and bent to kiss her.

'Did you hear me? I hitched a ride.'

'Loud and clear.'

'What constellation is above our heads?'

Ryan lifted his and pointed. 'That one?'

'Yes.'

'Orion.'

Amber closed her eyes and felt hands lift her body. Weightless and light as air, she floated listening to the din of the stars. Through the clamour and the shrill, she heard the words, 'Shine brightly. There is so much more.'

THE DOOR

Mike Moody

Herbert sat in his armchair staring at the door. He was next to the fire which, as well as heating the room, gave off a flickering light. This animated the door with moving shadows of distorted objects. It looked inviting, changing its appearance with the shifting firelight. It was almost like someone was waving to him, beckoning him to move on.

The noise of the rain knocking on the window told him it was still pouring down outside, but it did not dampen the warm invitation the door seemed to offer. It brought to his mind a river: the door was a spring; the street was a stream that led to the road, which was a river that led to an ocean, which was the world.

His shift at the mill had finished at six and he had walked home in the rain. Mary had made a stew and he had eaten hungrily as he always did after his ten hour shift. All was quiet. Florence and Arthur were in bed. They were both good children and he loved them greatly although he had little time with them. He thought of Florence, how she had grown a right little girl now, going to school. Tears welled in his eyes as he recalled her as a baby, his first child, and how he wanted the world for her; to grow up with a proper education and marry a good man who had some substance behind him. But how was that going to happen when his wage was just enough to have them all clothed and fed? She would have to leave school at the first opportunity and work in the mill just as he and Mary had, not to mention his brothers and sisters.

His thoughts moved to Arthur and again how overjoyed he had been to see his son just over four years ago. He was still too little to help with much around the house or go to school, but he seemed a bright lad with potential. But how would he ever realise that potential? They were all on a treadmill going nowhere; just stuck in a rut.

Whilst he sat contemplating, Mary, his wife of six years, was in the kitchen seeing to the pots. At least he was able to earn enough to let her stay at home and bring up the children, which was better than some families. His mother had done the same and her children had to start earning their keep as soon as possible to enable the family to have the essentials in life. His children would have to tread the same path.

His parents had given him a grand name, Herbert Hartley. Unfortunately his surname, Moody, let him down. Not that he was, at least not more so than anyone else. They had grand ambitions for him when he was young. His brothers and sisters had gone to the mill or in Frank's case down the mine. Either way there was money to be made, but it was money that wore you down with hard manual labour. His parents had seen in him an ability as a child; he had been to school and learnt to read and to do sums; he had even read books. However, they couldn't afford to keep him forever or send him to a better school, so at fourteen he had started work in the mill.

Most of the people in the street worked at Bulmer and Lumbs, it was one of the largest mills in the city. He started there as an apprentice Stuff Presser and now thirteen years later was still a Stuff Presser. Where had the years gone? When had his ambitions left him? Yes, he had a responsible job finishing off the woollen cloth, but that was not what he had hoped for when he started work. He had ambition and made an effort to improve himself through education, borrowing books from the Mechanics Institute. But at eighteen things changed, he met Mary, who also worked at the mill. She was four years his elder but was a stunner and she had smiled at him one day. That was it; he was caught, but willingly ensnared. From that first smile they moved on to an occasional chat and then meeting regularly outside work. It was all very formal at first but when he turned twenty one in 1904 they became very intimate and they married in April 1905. Florence was born in September and he was a husband and father with responsibilities.

His eyes and mind were still fixed on the door. It seemed to be calling to him. 'I'm here, an alternative life for you, just step this way.' He could just go out and move into a different world where he might achieve his ambitions. Of course this involved a risk and with two children and another on the way he knew Mary would not hear of it. She was too content with her rented house, her children, living near her parents and the church. No, she would not move away from her family and disturb the stability which she and her children enjoyed.

Mary's brothers and sisters had done well and didn't she let him know about it. Ernest worked for a law firm, Fred was trading wool and had already been on a trip abroad, and Rose was courting a wealthy businessman. Even her father was doing well having recently been promoted to a guard on the Great Northern Railway. The luck of the Irish! But her father had taken risks, travelling widely before he married and moving jobs and location after he married. The last time she brought the subject up he had blown a fuse and he could remember shouting at her, 'Why the hell haven't I done so well? Because I was stupid enough to fall in love with you and get married when I was twenty one. I've worked all hours to provide for my family and am now stuck in a job with nowhere to go; at least not in the mill. Shall I move jobs? What about moving to London? I know the answer to that. You won't ….' At that point Mary had broken into tears and he had softened his tone. They made up and Mary had not brought the topic up again, but he felt sure it would raise its ahead again, sometime.

Why had he been so stupid letting love, or lust maybe, take over his life and prevent him fulfilling his ambitions? It was 1912 and the world was buzzing, Great Britain was really great, ruling over vast territories all over the world. You only had to look at the atlas and note how much of it was coloured pink – the empire. Money was being made, Bradford was booming, as were most of the Northern cities, exporting goods to the four corners of the world. Yet here he was in a terraced house in Fitzroy Road, working in the same mill he had worked in since he was fourteen. Working hard, ten hours a day, six days a week. Except for that week in August last year when, after a prolonged heat wave through the summer and a drought, the mill closed for a week. They hadn't been paid, but the freedom! Oh! The freedom and the joy. It must have been that month that Mary conceived and now another little one was on the way, another link in the chain. The house and Mary were his ball, the children were the links in the chain that bound him to this existence and stifled his ambitions.

Herbert continued to stare at the door and was drifting to sleep.

'Herbert, can you come and help with this washing dear? I am eight months gone you know!'

Startled, Herbert opened his eyes. The door looked inviting.

He stood up, his heart beat quickening.

'Herbert!'

He walked toward the door and took his coat and cap from the coat hooks next to the door.

There were footsteps behind him.

'Herbert, what are you doing? You can't be going out now. It's late and you've got work in the morning.'

'Mary I'm not going out, I'm leaving.'

'What do you mean you're leaving?'

'I can't go on like this. I may as well be in hell.' His hand reached for the doorknob.

'No! Herb, no, please. I don't understand. What have I done? What of the children? We don't have a bad life. We need you.'

'Mary I love you all, but if things stay as they are that love will turn sour and so will our lives. You and the children will be fine. Your mother and father and your brothers are all doing well and will look after you.'

'But it's you I need Herb. Not them. Just think of the shame and hurt you are causing.' Mary broke into spasmodic sobs, tears running down her cheeks.

Herbert opened the door and as he walked out, without turning round, stated, 'It'll be for the best. I won't forget you and when I've made a success of my life you'll all share in it.' As he walked into the rain he could hear her wailing, but with each step the sound gradually faded until there was nothing but the sound of his steps on the cobbled street. With tears in his eyes he continued to the end of the street and turned into the road which would lead to the rest of his life.

HOLIDAY LET?

Joan Roberts

As you walk up the drive take care on the path
Slippery moss covered bricks that look like old bones
Trees bent, distressed in the agony of age
Crying your name, or is it just the wind's moans?

The house is so small, you expected much more
Lonely, unloved and the thatched roof so frayed
The chimney is twisted, crooked; askew
The woodwork is rotten the paintwork decayed.

There's no sign of life but you're forced to go on
Dead creatures remain from the feast of the Crow
Or some other dark creature hid from your sight
Who watches your movements the closer you go.

Your eye sees a flicker, a movement upstairs
A face at the window or a trick of the light?
The old door is open, inviting you in?
Or left ajar in a hurry as someone took flight?

In the garden a tombstone but no grave to be found
You feel movement behind you and as you turn around
A bite in your neck and you feel so much pain
You know that forever it's here you'll remain.

MISTAKEN IDENTITY

Joan Roberts

Sergeant Gregson stretched, yawned and removed his size 12's from the adjacent chair. It had been a long night. Inspector Gorse looked over at him. 'They've just picked up the girl,' he said. 'She's going through a line up now.'

'Thank God!' Gregson yawned, 'This has been going on for weeks!'

Myra sat in the interrogation room, the policewoman next to her, silent. Why was she here? They had planned everything so carefully, so clinically.

Brady said, 'Do it in daylight, it's less suspicious. Man and a woman, much less obvious than a man alone or two men. People don't notice a woman, trust her I suppose!'

Brady! Had they got him too? There was no way of knowing. They'd caught her? Someone saw them, the line-up, someone recognised her, how? Each time she changed her appearance, Brady too? That kid, the one in the duffle coat? No, surely they'd been so careful?

'Do everything naturally,' said Brady. 'Just go about as normal, and don't arouse suspicion'. She'd said this had to be the last time, it didn't feel right. It had been a laugh at first, exciting. Brady seemed different too. He was distant, less caring. He'd been great when her Dad died. Dad what a joke! The drunken pig, always knocking her about, she didn't miss him one bit. She'd been so grateful to Brady. At the time she'd have done anything he'd asked, she had; hadn't she? That's why she was here. Did they have him too, she wanted to know, had to know, but if she asked she'd give the game away. What weren't they telling her?

'Come on Myra,' Gregson looked at her across the table, 'just tell us where they are, give us an idea. Anyway, why should you take all the blame, we know you weren't alone. It'll be better for you in the long run if you tell us everything now. '

Had they got Brady? Were they just trying to trick her? She really needed to know. If he was with them now, what would he say? Perhaps he was tired of her, she was needy. Brady; he was like family, and without him, she could tell now, she couldn't even think straight.

Gregson stood and stretched. If he could put this to bed he could go to bed. 'Take her back to the cell and let her think about it'.

The cell was clean but cold, just a narrow bench with a plastic mattress, a thin radiator that gave no warmth. In the corner there was a bucket with a cloth over it. The policewoman caught her eye, 'It's for peeing', she said, in a thick Yorkshire accent, 'We've no mod cons 'ere'. The light was a long fluorescent tube in the ceiling right above her head, persistent and irritating; a yellow hue casting shadows on the grey walls. How could she sleep anyway, she could only think of Brady? If they hadn't got him then what was he doing, where was he? Would he run, leave her behind? If they'd got him, then what, what would he do, give her up? She was beginning to see what they'd done in a different light; this was trouble, real trouble. Brady had changed. He couldn't be bothered most of the time with her tales of her Dad and how he had been….

It wasn't her; she'd done it because of Brady. What if she did get all the blame?

Myra spread herself across the cold plastic mattress and put her hands to the back of her head. She couldn't rest from contemplating the future. Never in her life had she had control, it had always been someone else who called the shots. She kept thinking about what the copper said to her. He'd been kind in his way, as if he was trying to help. There was something in his eyes when he looked at her, was it kindness, concern? He was doing his job for sure but he seemed to think she had been used. Perhaps she could talk to him? She was tired, strung out. (You should be strung up, her Dad would say). But they'd been so careful, buried everything on the moor. What did they have on her? The moor, that desolate place, they couldn't have found anything there. Even she couldn't remember where they were buried.

Two more hours dragged by – she heard shouting from the other cells, drink, she knew the signs. That was one vice she didn't have. Dutch courage they called it – courage! It made you weak and stupid, it had killed her Dad. What a mess he was. She could use a cigarette. She craved a smoke, she could think, it would help her to think. She had told them nothing; but they had told her nothing. Surely they can't have Brady, surely not?

***

'I want you to do this, George', Gorse said to Gregson 'A paternal nature is what's required'. Sergeant Gregson was a big man but not overbearing, persuasive rather than threatening, he usually dealt with youngsters, particularly girls. The man they had in the other interrogation room was saying nothing. Didn't even have his name, they would get it, they were sure in time. He was bound to have a record. It was the girl they should concentrate on, he was a hard one, and she was vulnerable. 'Gain her confidence; let her think you're her friend. She'll crack, I know the type. The sooner we can get this sorted the better. A confession would make it a clean arrest, the evidence is good but a confession would clinch it'.

'Get the girl back in. Have another little talk now she's had a bit of time.'

Myra shivered at the key in the door, she must have dropped off. She followed the policewoman through to the interview room. The same copper was there as before. She took a deep breath and sat where she was shown. The copper introduced himself to the machine and everyone there had to say their name. Myra coughed slightly and her voice wavered. Gregson offered her a cigarette which she accepted gratefully. She inhaled the smoke and felt better. The interview resumed.

'You know you'll go to prison? What did he promise you? Marriage? He says it was all you, that you had stuff on him. That you look weak but you're cunning'. Her eyes looked at him, he had her, she was the right girl, she had been with him. 'He says you were always following him around, says you used sex to lure him in, then when it went too far, there was no escape for him. It was easier for you he says, to change your appearance. He said that people always seem to trust women'. That was it; he knew it was, that's how he'd used her. He couldn't have done it without her. She must have been vulnerable somehow, there was no family anywhere. Would she rise to it though?

Myra tried to hide her feelings' but she felt her stomach knot and sink. They have got Brady. She almost cried, and what's more he wants to make me take the major blame. She had relied on him for everything in the last two years; she was seventeen and enjoyed no life at all outside of waiting hand and foot on her drunken father and feeling his fist or his boot if she tried to get out. Brady had been kind, she had been vulnerable; she had been suckered in. Just when she should have been free to lead a new life, now she would be spending it in prison. Her whole life had been a prison up till now. She couldn't, wouldn't take the blame. If she told this nice copper everything he would help her, wouldn't he?

'I'll tell you,' she said, 'only you'.

'It has to go on record' he said, 'I'm sorry'. But believe me it will help your case to do this'.

***

The following day Sergeant Gregson read the report in the Daily Echo:
Myra Smallwood of no fixed abode and Brady Phillips, also of no fixed abode, were

charged yesterday with fraud and the theft of valuables, to the value of £16,000. stolen from various local homes. The couple posing as a cleaning company had been operating in the area for some time. Sergeant Gregson of Shady Lane police station is not optimistic about the recovery of the valuables. 'Trouble is,' he said yesterday, 'they've buried it all on the moor. We'll probably still be looking for it when they get out of prison!'

OWEN

Will Ingrams

First time I saw that lad he had no clothes on. Not a stitch. And out there in the middle of the street, wasn't he? And now I come to think, that was the same end o' January day I took Steph's boys up to visit Margaret with me. Their Grandma, o' course, but they don't see her so often now, not with her staying up in that Home. Visited her in that pokey little room, we did, no decent view or nothing. Bit depressing really. I wish Margaret was still here with me, like we always used to be, but she's not herself no more, is she? I can't look after her properly at home, can I? That's what Steph says, and I know she's right, really. What's that old song? Oh, Lonesome Me. Hmm. Sad old git, me, more like.

Anyway, I took the boys back home with me that afternoon, didn't I, 'cos Steph was off out with her friends later, the ones she still sees from her schooldays. Sally and Karen, I think it is. Didn't mind that though - that's just what she oughta be doing, with that useless Darren o' hers up an' gone now. She needs to get out and maybe meet someone new, don't she? But then I took the boys back to her late on in the evening, and that's why I was still up and dressed around half eleven, when I heard the commotion outside. I pulled back me bedroom curtains an' blow me, there he was. A naked man in the middle of the road! He was steppin' backwards along the centre line, all orange-looking in them streetlights, backin' off wary-like from a heavy-looking bruiser who kept kickin' an' slappin' at him, advancing slow and deliberate, looking for a big blow to bring him down. And this poor chap's bloomin' starkers - not even any shoes or socks - in that freezing winter night! No traffic that I could see, though you do often get a bit comin' out of town even near midnight, most Fridays. Well, that sort of thing's not right, is it? Couldn't let that go on, could I? So I opened me window wide an' I shouted down, 'Oi! Leave him be! That's not a fair fight mate!'

Well, the big guy didn't even look up - kept his eyes fixed on his quarry - but the starkers chap, he flashed me a glance an' he called out in a cloud of breath, 'Er.. D'you think you could you help me out at all, sir?' He had his hands held out in front, slightly crouched over, tryin' to protect his tender bits, looked like.

'Don't you even think about it mate!' shouted another voice, loud and threatening, and then I spotted two other young blokes, warmly dressed like the bruiser, tracking along with the action, mates of his, so it seemed. One of 'em was keepin' back the traffic, backing along the middle of the road and slowing them down, waving them away, and the second one was looking up at me, pointing his finger. 'Get back to bed, Grandad, and forget about it. All be over soon.'

Well, I could see how it was going to be over - that skinny shivering chap would be lying in the road with his head kicked in - so I hurried down the stairs and out the front door. I was still fully dressed, o' course, but I hadn't stopped for me coat, an' I could feel the frost in the night air as I stepped down me short front path.

'Hey, Grandad. I told you to forget it, right!' This chap had his head shaved almost bald, he was taller than me, and his tattooed arms were waving me back towards the house. Now I don't mind being a Grandad - I rather like it, really - but I wasn't *his* Grandad, and I wasn't gonna be told what to do by a three-onto-one bully boy either. So I made as if I was turning away towards the house, and when he looked back to the action I ducked past him and trotted into the road - the naked lad had retreated several yards past my gate by now.

'What d'you think you're doing? Let the poor boy alone. Where's his clothes?'

The big chap turned his scowling face to me just long enough to check that I wasn't much of a threat, then re-focussed on his quarry and growled, 'Fuck off home, old man. This guy's got it coming, haven't you McMahon? Get rid of him Scotty.'

My upper arm was grabbed from behind by the tattooed guy who must've come after me into the road - Scotty. I tried to pull away but he swung me round and I lost my balance, falling onto me hands and knees on the tarmac. Then things changed. I heard more voices, saw lots o' legs and feet running about, heard jostling and shouting. What happened, I soon found out, was that there were quite a few people watching - some who'd got out of stopped cars, some who'd probably been walking home - but they weren't doing nothing to help, just accepting the rule of those three bullies. When they saw me try to stop 'em and then get pushed over, they found their courage, I reckon, and started to get involved. Well, Scotty and the other two didn't hang around once there was half a dozen blokes steppin' in, and by the time I was up on me feet, brushing bruised hands on me trousers, they'd scarpered, and McMahon had trotted to my open door, hiding his nakedness in me front porch! Someone asked if I was all right, another person slapped me on the back, and then they were drifting away and the ugly little scene was all over, street and traffic gettin' back to normal. I hobbled back along the pavement, across the frozen flagstones to my door. To McMahon.

He was quivering and sniffing back snot, pulling my old gardening coat around himself, trying to get warm in the hallway as I locked and chained the door. He was snuggled up to the radiator, but that could only ha' been lukewarm, 'cos the timer switches off soon after eleven.

'I'll put the kettle on, boy, then we'll find you something to wear, all right? Don't suppose your clothes are nearby are they?'

He grinned through his shivers. 'Thank you sir. No, my togs're down behind the Queen's Head, in the bins. They made me take 'em off - pulled knives on me d'y'see?' His words were jerky and gasping because he was shaking violently from the cold and maybe from fear-relief. There was a bit of Irish lilt in his voice.

'I'm Bob, by the way. I'll put the heating back on for you, an' all.'

Five minutes later he was pulling on an old pair of my jeans and a thick workshirt, crouched in front of the gas fire in me living room. I'd given him some underclothes too, but everything was rather generous if a bit short - he was a skinny rabbit, but around six foot to my five an' a bit. None of my shoes were going to get onto those feet - looked like size tens at least. I put a mug of tea - with sugar - down on the arm of the sofa for him, sat back in the armchair with my own mug and looked him over, this McMahon.

He'd stopped shivering now, except an occasional shake and grimace - I'd seen some cuts and grazes on his dirty feet and ankles as well as his arms. His face was squarish for a skinny fellow, an' his wavy hair was all over the place - should have looked scruffy, that, but it seemed to suit him somehow. And he had pale blue, smiley eyes. Even when he'd been shivering half naked in the hallway he'd looked slightly amused by the whole thing. Those eyes didn't take life seriously, you could tell that. The stubble on his jaw looked like he hadn't got round to shaving for a couple of days, but maybe that's the way he kept it - can't tell these days, can you? He'd a bit of a pointy chin, so with that tousled hair and bright eyes he looked boyish, tall as he was. He took a swig of tea and sighed with a contented smile - you wouldn't imagine he'd just escaped a serious beating.

'I've got to thank you, Bob,' he said looking me in the eye and nodding. 'If you hadn't come out and interrupted Todd like that, it might've got nasty out there, so it might.'

'Looked nasty already to me, boy! Why were they after you? Wasn't a robbery, was it? An' I need to know your name too - I only caught McMahon?'

'Owen. And you got the last name right.' He grinned and I recall it seemed to make the room brighter. 'No, Bob, they just wanted me. All my stuff went straight in the bins.'

'Why then? You don't look like the type to pick a fight with anyone.'

'Ah now, you're right about that, Bob, I don't want any trouble. Todd, the big guy, he says I shagged his fiance. On her hen night, it would've been. He seems convinced.'

'Bloody Hell, Owen. I can see he might be upset about that. Do you know her then?'

'Oh yeah. Everyone knows Dawn. But I only kissed her that night, just for old times sake, so it was. We haven't had sex for a couple of weeks.'

'Shit! You serious, Owen? He's marrying this Dawn that you've been sleeping with?'

'Seriously Bob, he is. Myself, I can't see a future in it, but that Todd, he's not too bright about these things. I think it'll probably end in tears. But then I'll not be going to the wedding, anyway.'

'So he wanted to do you over, then, and got his mates to help?'

'Sure he did. Scotty and Def always hang around with Todd. They'll go along with him on his wedding night, I shouldn't be surprised.' Owen took another gulp of his tea, 'But he's had it in for me for a while now, since I took his job at the meat packing, and this hen night thing was a good excuse to go looking for me tonight. They found me just coming out of the Queen's, more's the pity.'

Owen seemed quite recovered now, the colour back in his cheeks. He looked at his hands and then at me, 'Do you think I might wash my hands, Bob? And maybe my feet too, if that's not too much to ask? I've got a bit muddy I think.'

I led Owen up to the bathroom and left him to get cleaned up while I found him some socks and then I went to get my spare wellies from the back porch. They're big for me, deliberate like, so I can get thick socks in 'em, and I thought they might just fit him. He came down the stairs humming a tune and tried the boots on.

'That's grand Bob! So I'll stroll down to the Queen's Head now, and see what I can find of my stuff before I go home. Would it be okay to bring your things back tomorrow, towards lunchtime? I don't usually get up too early on a Saturday.'

I said that would be fine, and asked if he was sure he'd be okay. I wondered if Todd and the others might still be looking for him.

'Ah no, Bob. He can't keep a thought in his head for too long, Todd can't. He'll have forgotten me by now - 'til he sees me the next time.' Then Owen took the old coat I offered him, thanked me again and slipped out into the frost and the empty street.

***

I was sowing me tomato seeds in the kitchen an' warming up the propagator when Owen knocked at the door with a supermarket carrier in his hand. He'd got home okay after findin' his shoes and his wallet from the back of the pub last night. The clothes, he said, were too soaked with beer and food scraps to bother with. The wallet had no cash left in it, but his cards and things were still there - a nice surprise he told me with a sparkly grin. In the carrier bag he had my old coat and jeans, but he said he was planning to wash the other things before he returned them - was a few days okay? Then he pulled out a six pack of Guinness - he hoped I could drink it. So I asked him to stay for a coffee and we sat in the living room just where he'd been shivering about twelve hours earlier.

Turned out that Owen had been in England since he left school a decade ago; he'd come over to find work - and he'd found all sorts by the sound of it. Only been in Suffolk since last Summer - stayed on after the Latitude festival - and he was living with a mate who rented in town. Owen was a bit of a musician, he said, and that made him plenty of friends wherever he went. He could play guitar and fiddle, but he only bothered to carry a tin whistle around with him - people generally lent him their instruments once they heard him play. We chatted about English and Irish music and some of the musicians I'd seen over the years - as far back as the Fureys and Robin and Barry Dransfield, who he'd heard of but was too young to have seen. I also ended up telling him about my Margaret. I think he must have asked if I was living on my own here and then it all came out. I probably got a bit tearful about it, 'cos I remember him putting his arm round my shoulders at some point. Anyway, he got his pipe out and played some tunes for me, and he was blooming good too - lots of sliding notes and twiddly bits. He knew some English tunes and was in the middle of Princess Royal when Steph and the boys arrived. Quite often she brings Daniel and Thomas round to see me on a Saturday - hopin' that I'll entertain them while she does her shopping. Gives her a little break I s'pose - so I wasn't surprised.

'Grandad! Look what I made at school...' Daniel broke off when he saw the stranger on the sofa; Owen had stopped piping when Steph let 'em in the front door ahead of her.

'What's that you got then Daniel? You can show Owen too - he's just visiting me.'

Now Daniel's a bit shy an' he usually stands tongue-tied and wary for a few minutes when he meets someone new, but something about Owen - his open face and twinkly eyes maybe - cut through all o' that. He went straight to Owen and showed him the miniature football pitch he'd made from a box lid, and its little lolly-stick goals with nets of gauze and all the white lines marked on. Then he set it down on the sofa arm.

'You go on the other side Owen, and blow the ball this way. Use this straw.'

Little Thomas stood watching the tiny ball buffetted around the pitch as Owen and Daniel chased it with their drinking straws. I didn't even get a greeting when Steph peered in after shutting the front door; she just goggled at them - heads-down and puffing away with enthusiasm, they were. She mouthed *who's he?* at me, then held up her hand to hold off the response, meanin' she was going to slip away without introductions and get on with her shopping. By the time she came back for the boys we'd all been over on the green with a real football for an hour and Owen had gone - but he was only allowed to leave after promising the boys he'd come round another Saturday to play with them again. I told Steph what I knew about Owen when she asked; the boys told her more as they ate the cakes she'd bought to go with our afternoon tea.

***

It must've been in March when Owen came to tell me he was off, 'cos I'd just potted out the tomato seedlings and was wondering what to do with the ones that wouldn't fit back in the propagator. You have to keep 'em safe from the frost, but gettin' a good light so they won't grow leggy. I had the Sungolds in little square pots so I could tell 'em apart from the Marmandes in the round green pots and the plum tomatoes in the red. You've got to have a system o' some sort, haven't you?

Owen said he'd got the offer of a job with a country folk band - just as a roadie really, but he was hoping he'd get to play a bit too. They were hitting some dates on the south coast, then going to Scandinavia for a little tour; he was quite excited about it, I could tell that much. He would be off the next day, that Sunday, and he'd called round to say goodbye and thank me again for helping him out that Winter night. Then he went on to say that he'd got a little surprise for me, and for Margaret, though he'd never met her o' course. Said he'd got to know a girl who worked in the office up at the Home, and she'd been willing to do him a bit of a favour. He hoped it would be okay. Then he gave me a big friendly hug and slipped out the door.

So when I went to see Margaret that afternoon I was thinking that I'd find some fresh flowers by her bed - or maybe a nicer vase for 'em than that plastic thing they'd given her. When I plodded into that boiled cabbage smelling day room, heart sinking as usual, despite the smiles from the staff on duty, I couldn't see Margaret sitting with the other inmates ignoring the television in the corner. Then Magda came over to me.

'Mister Pryke! Nice to see you here again. No, don't you worry, Mister Bob. Margaret is waiting for you in her new room.' And she led me off down the corridor and opened the door into a beautiful light room. Nice high ceiling, space for a couple of chairs and a table as well as her bed, and even French doors out onto the patio and the grass beyond! Daniel and Thomas could come in and out o' there and we could push Margaret out for walks round the paths, come Summer. My Margaret was sitting in one of the armchairs looking at me with more in her eyes than I could remember seeing for a long while, and seemed pleased to see me this time, to be reaching out to me just a bit. Well I have to say, I was so happy just then I got a bit tearful for a while, giving Margaret a bit of a hug, and Magda too.

'But Magda, how's this happened? And what's it going to cost?'

'I wouldn't know about that, Mister Bob. The office just told us to move Missus Margaret yesterday, so we did it. It's a nice room, this one, I think.'

It was. And she's still there now, without us paying a penny extra either. Margaret seems happier, more settled, and I visit her in a lovely bright bedroom, instead of that depressing day room which we had to do before - you couldn't sit in that pokey little cupboard o' hers for long. Owen certainly managed to make things better for us both, however he pulled it off. He was a bit of a wonder that lad.

***

Steph called round this morning, just as I was mixing up some feed for me tomatoes - they've set a couple o' trusses now, most of 'em. She'd didn't have the boys with her this time - they were at Audrey's, playing with her kids. Steph had something to tell me, she said, as I made the coffee. Took her a while to get to it, but then she told me she thinks she's pregnant again! Well, I was startled by that bit o' news I must say - I don't think she's even had a proper boyfriend since she sent Darren packing! Another grandchild on the way, eh?

So that's when I started thinking about him an' his twinkly eyes all over again. Seems like he might've done a bit more for us than I thought, that Owen.

SHIP OF FOOLS

Rosemarie Czarnocka

The boat moved slowly up river. It was a strange craft, long and narrow with a tree in full leaf for its mast. The rudder, with which to steer it, was fashioned from a branch of the tree. At the rudder sat a man dressed as a court jester but, in fact he was a hunter. In the bottom of the boat were some musical instruments, several flagons of wine and a large barrel of ale, together with a basket of fruit and delicacies to tempt the appetite.

The mud made greedy sucking noises against the sides of the boat as it drifted lazily through the dirty water, with the man at the rudder keeping a watchful eye on the riverbank. It was not long before he came across a group of three people, a nun and two heavily pregnant women barefooted and in rags. The nun was beating the two women with a heavy stick at the same time screaming, 'This is for your wickedness, take that and that.'

'You must be exhausted after punishing those wicked women?' shouted the jester. 'Come aboard, rest yourself, and take some refreshment.'

The nun readily clambered down the bank and into the boat. At the jester's request she helped herself to some wine and they made idle conversation as they continued on their journey.

Presently they noticed a monk sitting in the long grass watching a young boy gathering bulrushes to spread over the floor of the hovel where he lived with his widowed mother. The monk stood up and spoke to the boy. 'Come here, sit down and talk to me,' he said.

But the boy replied, 'My mother will be waiting for these bulrushes and I must go straight home.'

'I am a man of God,' shouted the monk angrily. 'Come here when I tell you to.'

The boy sensed this was very odd behavior and took to his heels and fled. The monk followed the boy but was hampered by his long habit and returned to his hiding place.

'Hello there,' called the jester to the monk. 'You must be very thirsty after that exercise. I have food, wine and ale and it would please me if you would join us.' The monk readily agreed and joined the nun and jester in the boat.

After a while they came across two men sitting on the riverbank. One was fat and looked very prosperous. He was enjoying his lunch from a napkin spread out across his knees. The other man was pitifully thin, dirty and dressed in rags. He was watching every mouthful hungrily and at last begged for some food of which there was plenty, but the fat man shrugged him off, moved away and continued eating his lunch.

'You could do with some ale to wash that food down?' shouted the jester. 'We have plenty on board, do join us.' He grinned as the fat man joined the other passengers.

The next encounter was that of two men fighting. They beat each other with their clenched fists and wrestled and seemed an equal match until one of them drew a knife and buried it in the other man's chest. Blood spurted from the wound and the victim sank to his knees at the murderer's feet. His eyes rolled back and he clung to the legs of his opponent only to be brutally kicked out of the way. He fell to the ground dead.

'We're going up river if you want a lift?' called the jester. It seemed as good an opportunity as any to get away from the scene of his crime, so the murderer accepted gladly.

Soon the jester spotted three farm labourers lying in a field of hay, which was waiting to be gathered. The men were laughing, telling jokes and flirting with one of the farm milkmaids instead of getting on with their work.

'Haymaking is thirsty work,' called the jester. 'We have food and ale on board and you are very welcome to share it.' The occupants of the boat were indulging in heavy drinking and carousing and the music was adding to the general merriment, which appealed to the lay-a-bouts. This was going to be much better than working. They all kissed the milkmaid goodbye, and ran to the river's edge to join the others and have a good time.

The boat continued its long journey, but everyone was too busy enjoying themselves to ask where they were going or when they would arrive at their destination.

As the sun went down the jester leaned back and took a long look at his human cargo. One of the farm labourers was lying senseless in the bottom of the boat while the nun leaned over him provocatively showing signs of frustration at his lack of response. Two men hung over the side of the craft. One was holding a flagon of wine in the water to keep it cool, the other tormenting two naked, starving men in the river by offering bread, and at the last minute, snatching it away. When he tired of his game he amused himself by holding each man's head under water until they drowned.

Everyone was drunk and soon became sleepy. The jester grinned and contemplated his hunting trip. It had been a good productive day and he felt very satisfied with himself. The boat's occupants had partaken of free food, free wine and ale and made merry all day, giving no thought to the price they were going to pay.

The sound of mirthless laughter echoed along the river as the boat disappeared into the shroud of mist and the jester spoke softly to himself, 'They all thought everything was free but they have paid with their souls which are now mine.'

TELL ME THE TRUTH

Judith Osborne

Mummy, being herself, said, 'Go ahead, smash my skull. I'll say what I want to say when I recover.'

Daddy, snatched-up paperweight in hand, was not himself. Not himself.

Nine-year-old daughter's terror moment went unremarked.

Daughter's steel-bound grip on survival at any cost, at all costs, slithered on unreliable surfaces of threatening serpent fears, but held, and held again. Held tightly and proudly into teenage, speaking then with unrealised strengths of poison, 'Go away, Daddy. We don't want you here.'

That was what Mummy wanted, wasn't it? So she would be happy, happy, happy. And if Mummy's happy, all's right with the world. Surely?

Please tell me that's right. Don't tell me otherwise.

Don't cry, Mummy, oh please don't cry again.

Daddy, smoker, consumed by cancer before sixty, at the furthest end of the country. Unaware remembered words of kindness to his child were noted, treasured.

How could that be?

Daddy just went away. Silent. Then dead.

A photo of his wife and little daughter was in his wallet.

Too late, Daddy.

Mummy crumbled, wept.

Don't cry, Mummy, oh please don't cry again.

Mummy passing eighty, beginning to understand that love needed to be spoken, even to a daughter, even by a daughter, crumbled, wept.

Too late, Mummy. Sorry. Very sorry.

REVENGE

Anne F. Clarke

'And so it is with great regret that we have to make you redundant.'

Frank sat bolt upright in his chair. What did he mean redundant! He was sitting in the Human Resources Office of the Scrumptious Potato Crisp Factory listening to the Head of Human Resources drone on about what a valuable employee Frank was and how the company really valued him and what a splendid job he did.

I should think so, thought Frank to himself, I've worked here for nearly forty years and I love my job. It is a really important role. Nothing would be the same without my input. It is essential to the product.

His mind dragged itself back to the HR office. What was the Head of HR declaring now? Frank had to concentrate hard.

'As a company we are improving our products, going forward, moving with the times' and 'I am sure that somebody of your experience and calibre can quite understand' and 'You will, of course, receive a generous redundancy package' and, worst of all 'We shall no longer need the little blue pack of salt in each packet, our crisps will be pre-salted!'

As Frank sat there whilst the Head of HR demolished his job, he felt a rising and dreadful rage, right inside himself. He screamed a terrifying scream at the top of his voice, picked up the paper knife lying on the desk and killed the Head of HR with it. It felt very satisfying.

Frank took the body down to the factory floor and put it in the potato slicer. Except for the right hand which he cut off, very carefully, and placed beside the vat of salt.

When the police came the next morning they found Frank and the Head of HR together, cut into neat slices ready to be cooked.

The little blue pack of salt had been tucked neatly between the fingers of the detached hand.

SURVIVAL

D. Green

Winded, Amanda curled into a ball and clutched her bruised ribs, desperately trying to draw air into her lungs. Tears of pain and fear poured down her cheeks. All those old memories forced to the back of her mind came flooding back.

'It will not happen again, not again.' Those words she repeated to herself daily, but here, now, he was so strong, so dominating, so angry that she could feel her courage slipping away, and self-doubt creeping in.

A man's figure drunkenly weaved above her. 'That's just a taster, bitch. Mustn't spoil the pretty face though, must we? Now get yourself indoors. I want money and then I'm going to have you. Thought you were clever changing your name, thought I wouldn't find you, well now I'm back to stay. Think yourself too good for the likes of me now your earning all that money?' Those slurred words were followed by another kick, which sent Amanda rolling across the cobblestone yard to land face down with something hard pressing against her hipbone.

A hand grasped a handful of her clothing, and dragged her upright. She didn't think just acted. She clutched for the jagged rock beneath her hip. He swung her round to face him and she let the whole of her weight carry through to her arm lashing out straight at his face. The rock smacked solidly against skin and bone and he released her with a squeal of shock, staggering even more, his hands to his face. The sickening stench of whiskey breath washed over her, but instead of retreating, she went forward swinging the rock again at his face. Feeling the bone give and the wet spatter of his blood across her skin.

Years of fear, years of looking over her shoulder gave strength to her arm and she swung again, feeling the skull cave beneath the rock and one of those hated, dark eyes that had smirked triumphantly down at her, popped from a shattered eye socket to lie wetly on a ruined cheek. He fell backwards his head cracking hard against the cobblestones.

***

'Cut', yelled Mike and was out of his chair clapping and whistling. 'By god girl, that was more than good. No need for a re-run, the emotion was astonishing. Best Actress nomination coming up.'

The rest of the film crew heartily joined in with the clapping.

Her co-star, Steve, stood up and rubbed off the red paste across his face with a towel someone handed him.

'Hell, Mandi, watch with the right hook, I've got a hell of a bruise on my nose.' He tenderly fingered his face.

Taking a deep breath Amanda dredged up a sunny smile. 'Sorry, Steve had to make it look good.' How could she ever reveal that she had lived through just such a scene in real life. There had been no need to act; her emotions had taken over as she relived every moment of that nightmare.

Across the set, Roger, the lighting man and her partner in crime for the past seven years, caught her eye and lifted an eyebrow. She gave him a quick smile. Roger had found her standing over the body. He had been the one to roll it in sacking and carry it to the pond beyond the stables. Then wrapped it in old, rusty chains from the plough shed, Roger dragged the body into the water sending the ducks flying into the sky. The pond now enlarged, was a wildlife haven and conservation area. The cobbled yard a walled garden harbouring vegetables, a grape vine, roses, and a hot house of orchids.

Their partnership started from that day, nothing sexual of course, not when she could still feel the weight of her father's heavy sweat stinking body sticking to her skin, and smell the smoke laden breath, and feel those short stubby fingers invading, pinching, thrusting up inside her.

She had despaired of bingo nights, because he would come and leave her crying among her dolls and teddy bears with those whispered words, 'Not to tell mummy or she would go away.'

Amanda brought herself abruptly back to the present with a shake of her head.

'Since it was that good Mike, do we get to finish early?' she asked her director.

'Don't see why not. Let's pack up people. Everyone back here 7am Monday morning.'

'Are you okay Miss Hammond, you're looking a bit, white?' Harry, the odd jobber who kept everything rolling and in place, including the actors, gave her a concerned look.

She took the hand he offered to help her down the stairs. Amanda waited for that nauseating lurch of her insides, the involuntary shrinking of her skin away from a man's touch, but instead there was warmth and strength in the firm hold on her hand; a sense of comfortable protectiveness as he guided her down the stairs.

Not dreaming then, she thought, for she felt the same last week when, with her arms full of script and a handbag, she had stupidly tripped over a lighting cable and Harry had grabbed her before she could land flat on her face. Calmly and smoothly she was placed in her usual chair as she had stammered out her thanks, her mind in a whirl.

Not like Roger, devastatingly, handsome, sexy Roger with his wavy black hair and roguish blue eyes. In the public's eyes the perfect live-in lover. Yet, for the sake of the Press, when he draped his arm around her shoulders or gave her a loving kiss on the hand, or worse her lips, all she wanted to do was vomit and run for the nearest shower.

'I'm fine thanks Harry. How are the kids?'

'Great. They send their love and I know I've said it before but thanks again for finding us Mrs Carstairs, she's a gem.'

'I'm glad it's all worked out well. Clara keeps phoning me to tell me how pleased she is to be out of that Home and in her own words, 'Being of use instead of twiddling her thumbs.'

Harry's young wife had died last year of cancer leaving him with a daughter of six and boy of eight to care for. Amanda removed one of her deceased mother's very capable friends out of a Home and into Harry's farmhouse as housekeeper/child carer.

'Ready, lover?' Roger's hand fell on her shoulder possessively. Amanda squirmed inside and kept a smile pasted on her face. 'We're going to the boat, plenty of sea air, fishing and sex.'

Embarrassed, Amanda shrugged Roger's arm away and rolled her eyes at Harry. 'Dream on. Sea air and I'm taking my script with me.' But really she needed to think, think about Harry, perhaps there was hope for her yet.

Amanda knew Roger had a woman, might even be plural, probably was, which was perfect as far as she was concerned. He was discreet, the perfect escort and appeared content to live his life around her acting commitments. Yet lately, lately he had become more greedy. In fact, just last week, she had caught him reading a bank statement and brushed her off saying he thought it was his. Two days later he demanded she replace his two-year-old Mercedes with a Porsche he just happened to try out last month.

When she had told him no, he had gone off into a sulk saying she could well afford it which she could now, but Amanda was a realist. She was at the height of her career with two Best Actress awards and three nominations under her belt. She gave herself at best another five years before her star descended and there was a new star arising on the block.

'Ready lover.' Roger slid behind the wheel of her Jag.

'It's been a long week. I'm ready for a relaxing weekend.' Amanda settled herself comfortably in the passenger seat and closed her eyes. 'I've a surprise for you when we get there.'

'A new Porsche?'

She could hear the eagerness in Roger's voice and grimaced to herself.

'All good things come to those that wait,' she told him.

Amanda thought about the surprise, a crate of wine, his favourite. Expensive and specially shipped over from France, a potent, heady vintage.

Roger was forever the glutton and after the third bottle would be legless. Everyone knew what a poor sailor he was and well, anything can happen at sea.

After all a girl has to look after her own survival.

TONY AND CLEO

Joan Roberts

'What a day,' Cleo said to Molly her assistant who was sweeping the floor. She looked round the shop. It looked devastated after the sale; the mess bringing back to her the shambles of her life. Her shop, her vision; it had begun like the answer to a dream.

Tony had been sent from his loan company to negotiate the details. It was a hefty lump sum, but she'd been sure she could manage the repayments. Tony was wonderful and she'd fallen for him then and there. He'd moved in, taken over really and things had been good, really good. He'd said he would get a divorce and they could be married. They talked about opening other shops. Then the trouble started; odd things someone setting fire to the car. Tony went missing for days at a time. Cleo suspected another woman or his wife being difficult over the divorce. Thinking back that would have been a much simpler solution. She felt as if she were under surveillance the whole time.

'I can't believe it Cleo, why did Tony do it? You must be devastated,' said Molly.

'I'm trying hard not to think about it. Somehow I've got to pay those bills or Octavian will foreclose on the lease. I've already had their heavies here; Tony said he'd deal with them. Quite honestly I'm frightened. I've got the VAT man on my back too. Thanks so much for helping out, you know I won't be able to pay you?'

'Don't worry. It'll take a while to find something else anyway. If the worst comes Mum says you can always have a bed at ours, until you sort yourself out. At least that awful man who was here this morning seems to have gone from across the street.'

Cleo looked out of the window to confirm what Molly had said. He'd been there for days now. His disappearance didn't make her feel any easier somehow.

'That's very good of you both. I'm seeing the bank manager in the morning after all it was Tony's gambling that got us into this strait not mine. I just hope they have faith in me. It was a good business, and all Tony's idea; oh my God!'

Molly ran over and put her arms around her friend.

'Have a good cry, just let it come out you must be exhausted. It was a good business and you are so talented I'm sure someone will help. You'll see Cleo's Garden will rise again. Can't you do a deal with Octavian, they did benefit from the good times?'

'Their business isn't run like that, I'm afraid. Leave it for now, I think I'm just going to close up for tonight, you get home.'

'What about the police? Surely if someone is threatening you they would look into it?' Molly looked at the blank expression on Cleo's face.

'People like Octavian aren't interested in the police, they're untouchable. They do what they want, when they want. No, somehow I have to raise the money and I'm afraid Tony has dropped me right in it! But, that's not your problem. Go home! You must be bushed?'

'Well we'll talk about it tomorrow. What's this? There's a handbag in the corner.'

'Oh, I clean forgot, never mind I'll open it later and see if there's anything in it with a name or address. Nice thing though isn't it? Beautifully woven pattern and lovely clasp, looks antique.'

'Sure you don't want me to do anything else?'

Cleo waved her away, 'Alright, I'll be off. See you tomorrow.'

'Yes bye and thanks again.'

Cleo put the bag on the wrapping table and went over to lock the door. She switched on the lights, but then remembered that the electricity had been cut off, and the phone. She had never felt so miserable and after all that hard work; she could happily have wrung Tony's neck. It had been so good, they had put everything they had into the business and Tony had done the deal with Octavian on the lease. How could he have let her down so much after all they had been through? Still, he must be at rock bottom now; the embarrassment when the police had arrested him this afternoon. At least they had done it quietly and he hadn't made a fuss.

She moved across the room, how quiet it seemed with the full moon rising in the sky and the failing light casting shadows across the conservatory. She noticed something moving across the wrapping table. She shrugged to herself, must be a draft blowing up the wrapping paper and she moved over to the door to make sure she had locked it.

As she reached the door she heard a noise behind her, the bag had fallen from the table. The door was locked and bolted, but she could still feel a draught from somewhere, so she moved across to the conservatory to check the windows, as she did so she picked up the handbag and placed it firmly back on the table. She also put the heavy tape holder on the wrapping paper to keep it from rustling.

All the windows were closed except one. Reaching up to close it she saw the reflection of the handbag in the glass where the last remnants of daylight were fading. It appeared to be rocking from side to side.

'What is the matter with me, I'm hallucinating now?' Shivering a little she bent towards the table as again the handbag fell on the floor. Picking it up she tried to look at the clasp in order to open the bag, but it was too dark. She walked over to the window and held up the bag so that she could see by the dim light from the full moon. It was quite beautiful, and she wondered who could have left such an obviously expensive bag and not returned for it. It suddenly felt as if something was alive inside it. It made her jump and she dropped it on the floor. She walked over to the light switch but no light came on. In her confusion she tried the switch for the outside lights but they too would not work. Looking back at the bag it seemed to be rolling from side to side. Thinking that something might be trapped in there she picked up a bamboo cane and prodded the bag. Now she was feeling a little ridiculous, she picked the bag up and walked towards the door in order to put the bag outside. The bolt would not move. She put the bag back onto the table and picked up the tape holder which she pounded against the bolt. She couldn't budge it.

Cleo began to panic a bit and chided herself for being so sensitive, 'I'm tired, the sooner I get out of here the better.' She picked up the bag and took it with her to the back office. She pushed down the bar on the emergency exit, but the door wouldn't budge. 'Oh God, the delivery man left all that compost right by the door and I forgot all about it!' The door to the office slammed shut. The window, she hadn't closed it! She felt around in her own handbag for her mobile phone. No signal! She slumped into her office chair and began to sob. On the floor at her feet was the handbag with the beautiful clasp. Cleo did not notice the bag moving and something slide from the bag to her ankle and round her leg.

Molly fell into her mother's arms and sobbed.

'It was a snake bite, some deadly foreign snake called an asp; they're looking all over for it.'

'How did it get in there?'

'They don't know. There was just a handbag by her feet and beside her where she fell was a business card with the name Octavian plc.'

'A PAGE TORN OUT OF TIME AND SPACE'

Judith Osborne

The view from the hotel window was breathtaking.

Hazel's mind and her permanently anxious grey eyes swooped over the pine-spotted glistening valley into the far peaks and up to the crisp blue heavens.

The last of the season's skiers were flies on the distant snow canvas, their movement barely perceptible. Her breath was taken away by the grandeur, but also by the extraordinary fact that she, and Don, were in the Swiss Alps. Not that they were here for the off-piste skiing.

It had been her idea. Her fingers curled as she thought back.

Less than a year ago, in Lancashire, she picked that photo out of the envelope postmarked Canada. That photo of the bottom half of Don's face.

'I'm living only half a life, you know. My shrink has been very helpful, but I haven't written any poetry since you left, and I hardly ever sing now. I've sent you this picture of myself, to illustrate how I feel. Why haven't you sent me a proper letter?' wailed the accompanying words on the page.

She groaned to her friend Rachel, 'It makes me feel so upset and uncomfortable, and what game's he playing?'

Rachel said smartly, 'A mind game, my love. Stay clear. Not good news.'

Hazel really didn't want to be remembering Rachel's warning when she was in an hotel waiting for Don to join her. But her memories were not biddable. 'Come with me and I'll see you all right,' Don told her frequently early on. She took this in the spirit of a pleasant shared jokey truth, but began to lose faith in shared concepts, when his virtuous-sounding quoting of 'The Truth will make you free' clearly referred to his own monopoly on the Truth.

He'd begun the marriage by kindly drawing attention to certain indispensable requirements, without which the happy carousel would not turn freely. 'Think of them as 'Fuhrerbefehl'. In fact I'll list them for you.' Hazel's German was up to knowing the translation was 'Leader's Orders', and it felt like a pretty blunt instrument with which to make his point. Worse was the unavoidable association with Hitler as the Fuhrer, which continued to make her flinch. The heavily identified events included, 'We go to the Library every Saturday' and 'Hugo (his son, then aged seven) saws firewood every day to strengthen his arms'. Faintly ridiculous as they should have seemed, somehow the Hitler bit made the whole setup more sinister to her, particularly when Hugo's occasional 'Please, Daddy, I don't want to saw logs or go jogging,' was overridden.

That nightmare dawn with the wailing ambulance dash came when Hugo reached 14 and slid into drug abuse, petty theft and trashing property, followed by an attempted overdose. Into the Alpine present came the jangling echo of Don's voice to the hospital's emergency doctor, while colleagues pumped his son's stomach, 'The boy's impossible to deal with. I've tried and tried, and nothing makes any difference.'

'No, no, - he's a lost boy and it's partly your fault, and you haven't tried hard enough. You're betraying him. That's not The Truth.' Hazel had wept, but only to herself.

Don was twelve years her senior and his son was his son and she was out of her depth and out of her league on every front. Teaching, socialising, music, sport, cooking, sex – all of them unequal playing fields on which he was the 'victor ludorum'.

Even his infidelities were beyond her, cloaked as they were in his romanticised version of himself with his adoring, beautiful, clever women, conveniently appearing whenever he was holding forth at a conference somewhere exotic.

She managed eight years, trying hard to 'do things right', but apparently not succeeding, then torn herself away a year ago, continuing to berate herself. Too soon to go! She'd thought. She'd believed in marriage for life. She had climbed in numb disbelief on to the plane in Toronto. Got off it at Heathrow exhausted, empty of all rational thought, self-awareness reduced to a murky whirlpool of distress about the past eight years, and trepidation about the future.

In the months of earning a living and replanting herself in her birth county came the gradual return of a degree of balance of mind. She was good at her work and she had friends. She got two Siamese cats, then a dog, and felt 'in a good place'. Then, wallowing in a kind of sauna of Dutch courage, from the liberation of no longer living with him, she had the urge to start looking for an exciting way to yet salvage something worthwhile from the wreckage of the relationship. An unstressed atmosphere of kindred spirits and mutual admiration two or three times a year, maybe? A state of wonderment for them both to experience?

Really? She had thought, and Really? again. Is that going to work?

'Well, for a start, sharing the magic of something like mountain grandeur should work for us. Other experiences have done – Lake Louise, the opera, the Hermitage Museum, St Paul's,' she'd told Rachel, who had smiled quietly.

Hazel found the details of the little hotel in Les Marecottes and nervously phoned Ontario with her suggestion. The prospect, Don made plain, did not excite. 'I don't understand. If you really love me, and you used to say you did, we should be living together for the rest of our lives and I would make you happy and look after you and see you right.'

She summoned up enough strength to repeat, 'I think we should try this kind of holiday first.'

Eventually he capitulated and the Swiss rendezvous was on. As usual she had ignored the necessity to be wary, really wary, of their differing expectations.

They spoke and kissed warmly, at their meeting in Geneva, and the little train up to Marigny was actually fun – a pleasant public sharing of something new, but she was still sweaty-palmed about his likely reactions to the hotel, to her, and to what she was trying to achieve.

Now the bedroom door behind her opened.

'Yes, well, this is an interesting place. What made you choose it?' The Scots-accented words carried the familiar overweighting of sinister implications, at odds with the faint, polite smile on the lips, which accompanied them. The expression in the green brown eyes, and the combative stance, indicated his real sentiment, 'Why on earth did you choose this place?'

She should stand up for her choice; she knew the place was all right. She mustn't allow the usual wash of embarrassed guilt about all her apparently stupid choices to take hold. 'I think it's perfectly nice, actually' she managed, dry-mouthed.

Immediately came back, staccato, 'Have you looked in the restaurant? Have you looked at the menu?'

She decided she'd be brave, not be drawn – he was so obviously waiting for 'a proper answer', a thoughtful, analytical critique type of answer. 'It's fairly busy, which it presumably wouldn't be if the food was awful.'

His authoritarian words clambered over hers. 'I looked at the wine list. Nothing of any real interest.'

Ah yes, the wines. Plus the Scotch before and the Scotch after. 'Isn't it a breathtaking view from our window? Shall we go for a walk? Then we can consider food and drink.' She hoped her smile was 'normal' and friendly, to encourage him.

'We could test out the bed first. We haven't seen each other for a year and I've missed you. Haven't you missed me? I always likened you to a classic Ingres nude, you remember?'

Yes, she'd found out how sleekly Ingres depicted his models and was flattered, years ago, when she was still a naïve and lonely student and he was the inspiring lecturer.

'Maybe after our walk?' she tried. No such luck.

His seniority of age and intellect, and Scottish single-mindedness, had always counted for more than mere reticence or reluctance on Hazel's part.

Half an hour later, crushed and warped yet again, she rolled off the bed away from him. What she really wanted was to walk on her own, see the scarlet and orange geraniums in the village chalet window boxes, gaze at far horizons among the mountain ranges, instead of at intimidating, near, fleshy outlines that she was commanded to admire.

That wasn't the kind of 'mutual admiration' between them that she was looking for. Leave him to sleep it off? 'Would you prefer to stay and snooze?' she asked politely. It had been known to happen in the past.

Fat chance.

'No, how can you ask that? I'm looking forward to hearing your views, as I always have done.'

Yes, 'entertain' him, to allow him to shine in his response and educate her.

There followed the prolonged Putting on of Clothes. At the hotel door, his first words were, 'Skiing wasn't invented by the Swiss, you know.'

Hazel's inward groan might almost have been audible, it was so heartfelt. Her contribution to the lecture, pushed to her limits a few moments later? 'Damn! I've just remembered I forgot to plant my mother's lobelia!' It did not deter him.

The resume of the development of skiing was followed by, 'Oh, I forgot to tell you I'd invited your friend the Family Court Judge for a drink – he seems to be my kind of man. I saw why you liked him. If you were back with me we could both get to know him better.'

Oh, lord – what next? He needed to prove he'd got the attention of someone she herself had liked. Also he was holding out treats to her, like sweets to a child. As if she'd give up her job and England to go back to the pit of snakes just to be able to talk to Geoffrey, however kindly disposed to her he'd been. Was there to be no end to the insidious mind games?

They'd reached the end of the village, and she and Don were at a fork in the road.

'Let's go through the pine forest,' he said, and there was enough sunlight through the branches to create a magic.

The track soon began to fall quite steeply downhill. Hazel's excessive nervousness of such slopes was legendary, so when Don issued the invitation, 'I'd love you to take hold of my shoulder and lean on me,' she did. Stiffly. 'Oh, look through the pine trunks at that setting sun! Just follow me off the track and in to the open. Let's try to get a clear view. Keep hold of me. 'I'll see you all right' – remember?'

Yes, nostrils flaring she remembered that promise.

And she was still leaning on him.

The unevenly sloping rocky outcrop beyond the pines gave an uninterrupted vista to the far horizon and the molten bronze disc of the setting sun, pinned to the sky by a bar of black cloud. The sky was a paler bronze around the sun. Geometric-edged shapes of distant pines were black cutouts, stage scenery, artificial drama.

Facing away from her into the last rays of the sunset he pronounced, 'I do like you leaning on me. I feel I rule the world, standing right up here,' taking a couple of decisive steps towards his kingdom, and the intervening space.

Without hesitation she leaned more heavily.

There was not even the echo of a scream from the surrounding peaks.

ARRIVALS, PEARLY GATES

John Antram

Just arrived: a furious man
With furrowed brow, white-knuckled hand,
Short-tempered, anxious, glaring
At the others who are there, and where
The ones in white command the gatehouse,
With their ancient scrolls and clipboards,
'See? He's one nerve short of a system.'
Peter Panzer.

To one side: a simple man,
Wide-eyed, curious, mildly bland,
Patient, glad to rest awhile,
But likely prone to stare at where
The ones in white command the gatehouse,
With consensual karmic clipboards,
'See? He's one feather short of a flight-path.'
Peter Pancake.

Then one other: green and strong,
Endangered in that Earthly throng,
Concerned in life to work for good,
To steward and to care, 'Just there,'
Say ones in white commanding gatehouse,
With their eco-tablet clipboards,
'See? He's one merit short of a miracle.'
Peter Panda.

DO YOU BELIEVE IN LOVE AT FIRST SIGHT?

Joan Roberts

It was 1941 and I was saying goodbye to Hunstanton where I had lived all of my 21 years. I was looking out across the green to the Wash, which remained stubbornly grey even in the July sunshine, and contemplating my past and my immediate future. The first months of the war had been filled with the skirmish of preparation and anticipation. By the end of 1939 they had begun to call it a phoney war, we were all ready but virtually nothing had happened. During April of 1940 the British Army had taken a battering in Denmark and Norway, and then there was the German invasion of France and the French seemed to give up, the result being that every possible boat had been used to go across the channel to try and bring back as many of our troops that they could. The evacuation of Dunkirk brought home to people just how serious a problem Britain had.

Then at the beginning of this year it suddenly seemed that our enemy was creeping up on us, sinking merchant ships in the Channel, North Sea and the Atlantic. Trying to cut us off and isolating us from Europe and America before invasion. Now we felt the war had truly begun and many of my male friends had received their 'call-up'; even women now between 20 and 30 were expected to serve in factories and on the land. I had decided to train as a nurse; it was adventurous for me after working in the little chemist since I had left school. My boss had been very supportive giving me a glowing reference and encouraging me. I know, however, that my mother was damming up her emotions when the confirmation came through the post. I was due to leave for London the next day to start my training on the following Monday. I had been a bit panicked by it all and had asked Mum to come with me.

'What would I do while you were training? Then they'd send you off somewhere and I would be left in London, knowing no one. No, I'll take my chances, thank you, among those I call friends. No doubt we'll be a comfort to each other. Now let's get you packed I don't want those there Londoners looking down their noses at my brave girl.'

I had hugged my mother and made an excuse to go down to the front before I became too emotional. I would have walked along the pier but it had been closed after the fire in the pavilion. I was wondering whether it would ever get rebuilt when a soldier stepped in front of me, startling me out of my daydream. He wasn't handsome particularly but his smile was warm and his eyes twinkled with mischief which, surprisingly, I found very attractive.

'Excuse me, do you live locally? I'm looking for this address.' I took a scruffy piece of paper from his hands which looked like an old travel pass with a penciled address that I was totally unfamiliar with, and suggested it might be in the Old Town.

'She definitely said near the green opposite the pier,' he looked dejected, 'or she may just have fobbed me off.' I felt really sorry for him; he seemed so pleasant, so friendly. I looked at the address again. I told him I had no idea where it was and when I looked back at him his face lit up with an enormous grin.

'I'm sorry,' he said, 'I made up the address as an excuse to talk to you. I've been watching you for a little while and well, to be honest I wanted to share today with someone, not just anyone, but someone pretty with a kind face, like you. My leave is up today and tomorrow I could be off overseas.' At first I couldn't believe his cheek. 'Would you keep a lonely soldier company before he goes off to fight?' He pulled a sad face with sorrowful, spaniel eyes and though I would probably have advised anyone else to refuse, somehow I couldn't. After all there was a war on and I really needed the distraction and honestly, where was the harm?

We had quite an afternoon in the new fairground and Holiday Park. We shared a pot of black tea and a couple of dry scones with the tiniest piece of butter in a little teashop. His name was Albert Jenkins and he was from Manchester and had been brought up in a boys' home. He had been sent to East Anglia to do his army training and came to Hunstanton when the others went home on leave. We laughed as he described the other men in his unit who had become his best friends. We walked along past the boating lake and the bowling green. Then we sat quietly on a bench contemplating the future and what it might hold for us both.

'I'm not so much scared,' he said as he took my hand, 'as lonely I guess. There is no-one really who is here for me.' He put his hand on his heart. 'I don't really feel any reason to come back; my life is with them now, the boys in the unit.'

'Let's not be maudlin,' I said. 'We will be right in the middle of an adventure, especially you. It's incredibly frightening but exciting too, don't you think?' I really felt we should be positive.

'I'm glad you said you'd come with me today you've been great company, Lucy Fuller, it's a pity there's not much time.' He kissed me then; my first real kiss. I responded to his warmth and his loneliness, he would kiss other girls no doubt but this would be his last kiss here, something to remember when he was out there fighting for his country.

'Let's make a pact,' he said suddenly, 'to meet after the war, here at this point on the same day, July 18 in the afternoon.'

'Yes,' I said, 'we should meet again. I was going to suggest writing anyway, I know where I'll be living and…'

'No,' his face was beside mine, his eyes were warm and tender. 'Let's take today with us and both of us get on with whatever life has to throw at us. I can't bear the thought of someone waiting, hoping about me, it's too much responsibility. I don't know what's out there for me. I know what I've had today though, and I can take that with me. Do you understand?'

'Yes I think so. This is really it isn't it, for both of us?' I shuddered a bit at the prospect of what may lay ahead. Nothing was certain, even the bench we were sitting on might not be there in however much time it would take for this to be over. We sat for a while in silence just looking out to sea as the sun started to go down and I realized this might be the last time I would have this view. Then we walked to the station and that was it, he was gone and I went home to finish packing.

***

I remember VE Day like it was yesterday. Suddenly the war in Europe was all over. It was hard to believe. I worked a night shift at the hospital in Kent where I was transferred after my first year's training. Becky wanted to go into London to celebrate and, well, it was such a special day I could hardly refuse. We laughed at a sailor who climbed a lamp post calling out to a young lady he had his eye on. There were couples kissing everywhere and other people dancing to someone playing a squeeze-box and 'Roll out the Barrel'. The war had changed everything. My mother moved down to be with my Aunt Cissy in Essex, when she was not only widowed but had lost both her sons, one in Africa and one in Italy. I was going to work in a hospital nearby in about another three weeks.

'What now then Lucy? I'm looking forward to seeing Jack again; we'll get married as soon as we can. Let me have your address so I can send you an invite.' I was pleased for her it hadn't been easy for Becky and she lived for any news she could get of Jack. We spent the whole of one weekend in church praying for him when he was missing.

***

After a few weeks I settled in with Mum and Aunt Cissy. I promised myself that I was not going to spend the rest of my life with them, somehow I would get out, maybe go back to London. I didn't allow myself to think about 18th July as I was convinced that he would not be there. I met many young soldiers, sailors and airmen during the war and enjoyed their company but my mind always went back to Bert and that afternoon and evening we spent watching the sun go down together. Even though it had not been my initial intention, I found I was using it as an excuse not to tie myself to anyone. As the time grew closer I thought about not going. Had it been a romantic dream, he'd probably forgotten all about me? I nursed many badly injured young men and witnessed the heartbreak on both sides when wives and girlfriends were confronted with the consequences. Becky's boyfriend had been missing for a while; it was hell for her. Previously handsome young men were disfigured, lost their sight or lost limbs; their sweethearts unsure whether they were feeling love or pity? I had no idea how I would react in such circumstances. Then there were those who would never return; I couldn't bear to think about it. The plan was that neither of us would be bound to the other, in case anything happened, but I did feel bound; afraid to meet him and at the same time longing to see him.

I booked into bed and breakfast accommodation for three days, it was extravagant but I could spend the time catching up with old friends. Everyone would have plenty to talk about and it would help me to get over the disappointment of him not being there. I did my hair especially to look as it was when I met him the first time, although it wasn't quite as long, and I wore the same dress. A wartime diet certainly helped with the waistline. I felt both nervous and a bit silly; after all we'd met one afternoon four years ago and hadn't seen each other since. My experiences had been dramatic to say the least in the meantime and there was no way to know what terrors he might have been through.

As I walked towards the bench I could see someone sitting there, a man holding on his trilby hat because of the wind. My heart was beating practically in my throat so I took a deep breath and went closer, gulping down the butterflies in my stomach. Hearing me approach he turned round and I caught my breath. It wasn't him. I felt suddenly devastated, dismay flooding through my veins; I steadied myself with the back of the bench. I couldn't help it, the pain of disappointment was so great; I tried to stop the tears but I wasn't doing a very good job. I apologised clumsily and tried to explain that I had been expecting to meet someone. The man got up from the bench and smiled sympathetically.

'I'm sure he'll get here if he can,' he said and left. I took my handkerchief from my bag and sat there looking out to sea wondering about these very emotional feelings going through me. He might not have even been DE mobbed yet, unless he was badly injured. How would I feel about that? I knew though it wouldn't make a bit of difference. I'd done so much thinking about it recently and all I really wanted was for him to survive so that I could see him again. I would do everything I could to find out what had happened to him; there must be a way and for a moment it helped to suppress my terrible disappointment. I sat for a while as the sun started to set above the sea, just as it had all those years ago; the memory became too painful and I decided to walk back to the B&B. I glanced across at the pier which they had started to renovate and I thought I heard someone calling my name.

'Excuse me, could you direct me to this address?' I turned as someone seemed to tap my arm and I could not believe my eyes. Bert stood in front of me in uniform, puffing and panting as if he'd run a marathon. I threw myself into his arms and completely broke down; I didn't notice anything about him, just that he was there and still alive. 'Trains were a nightmare, I've come up from Portsmouth, thought I'd never get here.'

It was some time later that I saw the scarring and we spoke about some of the terrible things he had witnessed. When he awoke screaming in the night, I was so glad to be there to comfort him.

DOCTOR UNDRESSING

John Antram

Wearing a freshly laundered house-doctor's coat I entered the private room in the hospital. Nurse Matthews, who had been arranging furniture and placing equipment beside the Lady Jessica, was ready to pass me some rubber gloves. Our patient was calm, her discomfort eased by some concoction prescribed by the personal pharmacist who had visited earlier that morning. She knew I had arrived slightly earlier than the appointed time but signalled a welcoming acceptance. Nurse Matthews excused herself to attend to another matter further along the corridor.

'Come over; let me hold your hand a moment,' said Jessica. 'I can't see you or say very much. Talk to me.'

'My Lady,' I said, 'I am forever in your debt. Who knows how long I would have lain there if you had not rescued me? Almost certainly I owe you my life.'

'We've been over all that.' She spoke languidly, her head swathed in bandages. Her hand tensed its grip. There was a brief silence, and then she spoke again, 'How are your lungs now?'

'I am fully recovered, thank you. This morning I told the cabbie to let me out half a mile from St. Bart's and then I ran alongside the hansom to the hospital.'

'You fool!'

'No, I had to stay with the cab as my case of instruments and several books were still on the seat. But he did drive slowly the last quarter mile. He's a good man and brings me here from Barrington Street most mornings. We will begin to unwrap your bandages when the nurse returns.'

'Not the kind of present I would gladly give you, my darling.' Jessica suddenly drew in her breath. She must have heard Nurse Matthews' returning footsteps. I relinquished her hand then to don the gloves. Had I known exactly how long the nurse would be away I would have planted a kiss on the lips of my patient. As it was I sat near the bed again and reached for the scissors.

Trying to lighten the atmosphere I said, 'Let's begin to unwind,' and began to gently dismantle the outer bandage. The dressings beneath would require the steadiest hand ever and, although my touch was sure, my concentration with eyes and hands coordinated by training, another part of my brain reflected on the poignancy of it all. Much of the history I had learned after the event from the janitor of the Barrington Street building in which my consultancy is based. The curtains at my open window had caught the gas lamp. At my desk, with my nose buried deep in some medical tome, I had not noticed until nearly a whole wall of the panelled room was alight. It is thought some kind of varnish on the Chinese bureau caused the fumes which overcame me as I fought the blaze.

I removed the complete outer bandage from Jessica's head and began on the next, choosing first that which covered her eyes, enabling her to watch me as I worked on the remainder. This, I hoped, would give me strength to come to terms with the scarring that would be uncovered.

Apart from the commonplace, there was little I could say to Jessica while the nurse was with us. I wanted to say how I would love her more than ever; how my window had been open so that I would hear when her cab arrived; how quickly I would have whisked her from the consulting room to the bedroom; how, even now, no-one at the hospital is aware of any special relationship between us.

Lord Mantringham, Jessica's husband, is an influential patron of the hospital. For his much younger wife to be indiscrete with one of the staff would create a citywide scandal and some serious failure of funding. In addition, I was soon to have a meeting with Mantringham and others, to discuss the detailed costs and allowances for my specialty training. My particular interest in neurology had the support of the committee, but recent events had awakened in me an urgent wish to study an altogether different discipline. I felt Mantringham, in particular, would support my change of proposed choice.

'This may sting a little,' I said, reaching for the tincture of Beech tree. We wiped and worked, Jessica's eyesight was restored; we drew the blinds closed and she looked at me in that way I had grown to adore.

'You look worried, Dr. Penrose,' Jessica of course addressed me formally, 'and at least five years older.'

'That's the effect of the smoke,' I said. 'I must have lain near that door for ten minutes. I'm so glad you were not late.'

'I hope your sight will not be stung by what you see.'

'I've not seen Mr. Reynolds's work in a case like this,' I said.

Jessica had arrived punctually for the chiropody pretence we had cultivated. I have no memory of Jessica's pulling me from the smoke or of the explosion of a brandy decanter while she dragged me towards the door. The Janitor had arrived in time to help us both to safety and to summon assistance. He dealt with us, and the fire, in an exemplary manner. Naturally we were both taken to St. Bart's' and I was working as normal again within three days. I could not participate in the emergency treatment of my lover's injuries. The sewing and patching had been done by Mister Reynolds, the most senior surgeon in the hospital, with Mantringham more or less looking over his shoulder. Knowing Reynolds' drinking habit when no emergency was expected that evening, I could imagine a hurried procedure had been executed with an unsteady hand.

It was only fitting that later I should supervise the day by day attention of Jessica's injuries. They were mainly wounds to her face and hands. One large fragment of glass had gashed much of one cheek, which would surely need further dressings after this inspection.

My delicate unwinding of the bandages revealed the full extent of the injuries. Superficial cuts were healing well, but the major damage resulted in a horrific grimace; stitches had puckered the smile-line into a ghastly rictus. The drooping eyelid, the misshapen ear and the scarred scalp, were now assembling into a horribly disfigured version of the woman I had worshipped. How could I continue to love her?

There may be an answer within the growing discussion in the journals these days, not only how neurology is garnering increased interest, but also how recent experiments and results are exciting in a new specialisation, that of cosmetic surgery. If Mantringham and the committee agree, I can study and improve on my subject to my heart's content. The Lady Jessica will be given every opportunity to visit my room; an arrangement which I trust will also be to her heart's content.

THE MALE SWAN

Joan Roberts

It had been a really busy season and I was exhausted, another dancer and I had shared a taxi to the station and he helped me lift my heavy suitcase up onto the luggage rack above the bench seat and had then made a dash for his own train. It looked as though I might get the carriage to myself, lucky me. So I stretched out on the bench and fell sound asleep.

I woke up suddenly for a moment unaware of my surroundings. Opposite me sat two young men, dressed in expensive looking black suits. One of them seemed amused by my dilemma.'Es tut mir leid.' I apologised in my inadequate German as I sat up; moving as close to the carriage window as possible, my embarrassment increased as my handbag, which I had been using as a pillow, fell on the floor. I looked into two of the bluest eyes I had ever seen as the amused young man bent forward to retrieve it for me.

'You are English I think?' he asked and then I think he said something like his name was Karl Becker and he mentioned his colleague but I didn't catch the name; I don't think I was that interested in his friend. 'We got on at Stuttgart and we are going to Ostend and then to study English at Birmingham.'

I felt a sneeze coming on. I did have a terrible cold but I think this was brought on by pure excitement. 'Hello,' I sniffed, 'I'm Helen, Helen Hunter. I've been staying in Munich, where I've just finished my first season. Ballet, I'm exhausted from Swan Lake! That is why I was sleeping. Ahtishoo!" Was there to be no end to my embarrassment? I took the immaculately ironed handkerchief from him with the beautifully embroidered K in the corner and apologised again, both for condemning him to a dreadful cold and also for my poor German.

'Your German is excellent,' he said, word perfectly in English. 'I love the music from that ballet; do you know Tchaikovsky arranged it around just a few notes? So many different tensions and inflections, he was a brilliant musician, don't you agree? How long have you been in Munich?'

'A few months, I'm on my way home now for a few weeks. My parents will be meeting me at Victoria.' Why was I telling him this? He was obviously educated and judging by his clothes quite well off, and me prattling on like a child. I brushed my hands down my jeans as if I had crumbs on my knees and tried to hide my scruffy trainers under my leg-warmers. He gave me another reassuring smile and told me that he spoke 5 languages; I can't remember them all, but that his English was not as good as the others, hence the visit to England.

We talked on about the ballet and I tried to tell him as much about England as I could, I knew nothing of Birmingham but I told him a lot about London where I had studied with the Royal since I was eleven. In fact I felt conscious of the fact that I did a lot of the talking and he looked at me smiling that beautiful smile, pretending to be enraptured by my every word. Too soon we arrived at Ostend. I started to reach for my huge case and embarrassed myself once again as my coat landed on my head. A sudden fit of sneezing afflicted me as I felt his arm on my shoulder to help me free myself, and he lifted my case down. Then we laughed as I struggled in my handbag for my passport, he of course just put his hand to his breast pocket and had all he wanted.

'Oh, now where's my ticket?' I fussed. He carried both our cases and it was as if we had planned to journey together.

As the train slowed into Victoria my heart began to sink but I couldn't suggest anything about meeting up. We lived miles from Birmingham and I had been away for months. Mum would have missed me so much. I was so tired, from the dancing and the journey and by the time I found Mum and Dad I was completely exhausted. I introduced him, as he had insisted on carrying my case and we shook hands, did his hand linger on mine? Or was I clinging on to him? By the time I reached my Suffolk home the whole incident felt as if I had enjoyed a wonderful dream.

***

A couple of weeks later I received a letter. I had no idea who it was from and when I opened it and saw this beautiful gothic script I knew at once. He explained that he had made a note of my address from the label on my case, and hoped I didn't mind as he had not been able to forget me. I read it over and over, and I held the paper to my nostrils to see if I could smell him to make it real. He lived near Stuttgart but his sister lived in Munich and when he could he would combine a visit to her and to me and with my permission perhaps we could go out to dinner, if our calendars allowed. Yes I thought, oh yes and I ran downstairs to find writing paper and envelope. Then to my utter despair I realised he hadn't given me a return address. I slumped on the bed and read the letter again and again but there was no clue. The postmark was Birmingham, which didn't help at all.

'Want to go for a drink Sis?' cried my brother who was apparently fulfilling a request from a friend of his to introduce me as I found out later, and so by the time I was back in Munich it really did seem as if I had imagined the whole thing.

Rehearsals for the new ballet had gone well, but the point work had been complicated and I hadn't been the only one kept back after dress rehearsal. We were all discussing each other's short comings when someone said that there was the dishiest guy asking for me at the stage door. As soon as I could get away I ran to the back of the theatre and there he was with the most enormous bouquet of flowers in his arms.

We were together as often as 'our calendars would allow' during the next few months. He took me to dinner at the very best restaurants and he invited me to meet his sister and her husband and two children. I was dancing on air. He obviously had a tremendous relationship with them all and I couldn't help thinking what a wonderful father he would make.

One evening I think we were both ready to take our relationship to another level but suddenly held me at arm's length and I couldn't understand what it was but he became very thoughtful and distant.

'I'm on the pill,' I pleaded.

'I have to go,' he said. 'I must catch the train tonight. I will call you tomorrow.' He kissed the top of my head and left.

My heart felt like a brick in my chest. I had no idea what was wrong. All through the night I questioned myself, and chided myself. I kept thinking about his sister, I felt certain she would have said if he was married. There were occasions when we had been talking and she had stopped abruptly as if she had said too much or was about to say too much. My bewilderment continued for days. Thanks to the performances I couldn't give in to complete heartbreak, and I was very tired at the end of the evening so sleeping wasn't a problem but every spare moment was spent either telling myself off for making my feelings so plain or wondering, questioning every sentence he had uttered to me. I knew he loved me, I knew he did. He had phoned the next day but I felt that thoughtful distance again in his voice.

I was looking forward to a visit from my mother; I had been frantically arranging things between rehearsals. Karl would meet her at the station and bring her to tonight's performance of Swan Lake. Apart from their brief introduction at Victoria they had not met before and I hoped they would recognise each other. I felt confident that my mother would get to the bottom of whatever was wrong, if anything but I also made up my mind that while she was around, for moral support, I would confront Karl about things even though my heart skipped a beat at the thought.

'Helen, wake up it's our cue,' one my three cygnet sisters grabbed my elbow as we entered for the 'Pas de Quatre'.

Afterwards back in the dressing room a small bouquet sat in front of the mirror and there was a card in beautiful gothic script simply saying: Your Mum and I are great friends and are at the stage door. Karl x

We had a wonderful evening and across the table my mother continually shot me glances of 'you lucky girl' and 'what a catch!' She was nearly as taken with him as I was. After dinner we walked in thoughtful silence to the small hotel where I was to stay for the few days of my mother's visit. Mum made her excuses and went upstairs to bed.

'I'll be up in a minute,' I said, handing her the pretty little posy from the theatre. Karl put his arms around me and nuzzled his chin in my hair.

'I need to talk to you about something,' he said. My heart skipped a beat. Was he going to break up with me? Perhaps he had decided to ask me to marry him? I looked up into his face, he was ashen, concerned, and there were tears in his eyes. 'I feel like the male swan that is in love with the Princess. She can never be his, she can never live on the lake and he cannot leave it.' He swallowed his tears as he explained. 'I am a Jesuit scholar; it has been my life since I was 14. Soon I have to make the decision whether to make it my future. I will have to choose between you and a life of service to God.'

I was so stunned I couldn't speak. I had never even guessed that this was the kind of problem he had been grappling with. I didn't understand about being devoted to a faith, I knew nothing about the Church. I looked up into that handsome face fighting to take control of his feelings. The tears were streaming down his cheeks.

'Do you hate me?' He gripped me harder and I too started to cry as my whole world came apart. I shook my head muttering between my sobs. 'You have made up your mind?' I asked. 'You waited till my mother was here so that I had someone with me?'

The tears dripped from his chin as he nodded. I realizsed that it might be the same if I had to choose between him and my dancing, which meant absolutely everything to me and I began to understand something of what he must have been going through.

He kissed me then, the softest warmest kiss I have ever had. He turned and left. I never saw him again.

COPY, COPIER, COPIEST

John Antram

When I was delivered as a new photocopier to this office, I was placed over a weekend next to an ancient machine I came to regard as my mentor: Old Gestetner. I wish we had longer together he knew there was not a great deal of time in which to tell me of all the knowledge he had accumulated. He was keen to make me aware of my place in the scheme of things.

'Xerox,' he said, 'you may be a smart new piece of equipment with programmes and circuits of which I cannot begin to conceive, but like me you need a life force, an energy, in your case electricity, to function properly and do your work. I may be a noisy, dirty, old thing but once I was 'state of the art'.'

He went on, over that weekend, to recount a history of our tradition, of which I had not been made aware until then. It was as fascinating as it was inspirational.

'We are the present-day embodiment of the spirits who now enjoy their afterlife,' he said. 'They labored through centuries, often in harsh conditions, to satisfy their masters or overlords. There were people with chisels on stone; scribes, monks or ledger clerks with quills, pens or brushes, on parchment or paper, copying or taking dictation. Then Caxtonistas, of course, with their revolutionary gear wheels and presses. All have had their part to play, bringing messages and meanings to increasingly larger audiences.'

In addition, he theorized how the sequence of change in these techniques was accelerating, how he had become obsolete in just a few decades and would soon be enjoying his own afterlife. He predicted correctly that my own working life would be shorter than his.

On the Monday, when Old Gestetner was taken away, I had much to occupy my mind, but soon I also had the unexpected distraction of a new water-cooler placed next to me: the gorgeous Fontana. Over the next few years we were together, and it was a wonderful partnership. By day we were industrious and helped the office to function smoothly in a multitude of ways. By night and over weekends we could compare notes about office intrigues, romances, promotions, parties or disasters; all the gossip was exchanged.

We had our romance too. We shared a double socket outlet and our back-up circuits could experience the tingling frisson together when not otherwise occupied.

There were some few early warnings of my impending redundancy. The service repair man had to visit me more frequently. I prepared my farewells to Fontana by recounting all I could remember Old Gestetner had told me, and I'm so glad I did. A new Swark-Chi was delivered. I learnt it (he or she?) has a digital heart which connects with all the office computers; it can sort, stack and file copies far more competently than I ever could. I was disconnected from our socket and, as I was carried away, Fontana promised to pass on my words to Swark-Chi.

Now I can rest in this new space and commune with the monks and scribes of old. Below, I still hear the bustle of the everyday world, but it's more peaceful here in the dusty afterlife of the office attic.

TIME

D. Green

Dark velvet skies ruled by a silver crescent.
A handful of sparkling stardust scattered across the blackness.
Silence within the great void.

A sliver of dappled light flowing upwards and outwards claiming the darkness in a splash of vivid blue.

The chattering of birds startling across the great void.

Daybreak.

RAINY DAY

Will Ingrams

Great. Another wild, wet morning.

 Still under the quilt in the February darkness, Dan listens to the deep flutter-whoop of gusty wind in the chimney, the mouse dance of hard rain on the plastic windowsill. He can almost feel the mud thickening out there, waiting to squelch round his shoes so it can smear itself onto his trouser legs when he squeezes behind the steering wheel. Hmm, arrive for the meeting with straggled hair, rain-stained shirt and muddy legs won't you, you bloody scarecrow?

 Last night's woodsmoke traces creep into Dan's consciousness on the expanding tick of the storage heaters, reminding him that it will be cold outside, even without a proper frost yet this winter. Better get Katie up and dressed warmly for nursery, then some microwave porridge, perhaps, before battling out to the car. Tough start, with Liz away, but at least she'll be back tonight. Go on, you lazy sod, get up.

***

 Katie swirls another dollop of plum jam into her porridge puddle. 'No toast, Daddy. Full up now.'

'You sure, K? You can eat it with Cbeebies on while I get ready, if you want?'

'Okay. Just a tiny slice,' as she slides off the chair, remote in hand to banish the morning news, 'with peanut butter!'

'Please, did you mean?'

'Yes.' Long silence, Dan's raised eyebrow eventually observed, 'Please, Daddy.'

 Dan snags the last toastered slab to spread for her, catching glints of the outside porch light refracted in by the fat raindrops on the black windowglass, quivering in windblast.

***

Leaning in to tight-click the child straps, Dan feels ankle-pelting rain soak into thin suit trousers. Kisses Katie's nose before pulling up his hood again, and dodge-slams the door in one smooth move. She sees him sideslip into the seat ahead and struggle to shuck off his wet coat as it clings longingly to headrest, steering wheel and then gearstick before it can be dumped. Engine running, but no heat yet, Katie shivers, watches steaminess cover the window insides and, as the courtesy light fades, dim shivery rain beads on the outside.

'Be warm soon, Little K,' Dan calls back to her as he twists lights to bright and pulls away from the cottage. Rain dives diagonally through the beams as they pause before Dan swings them right into the narrow lane, no headlights approaching. Up the hill through water coursing down, right at Charlie's place. There he is, silhouetted in the porch light, hooded raincoat flashing highlights as he bends to tug his blown-over wheelie-bin, dark dog waiting beside him, slow wag of trailing tail. 'See Charlie and Yoda, K?'

Katie turns her head to look, but the kiddie seat edge stops her seeing back. Just the dark wet window. Dan turns them left down towards the ford and the long twisty lane to the main road. Bare branches broken on the road, low twigs tossing fingerlike in the headlights, wipers double speed. Half a mile to to the ford - usually dry concrete with stream channelled under, but not this morning.

'Shi.. iver me timbers, Katie! Stream's high this morning, all right!' Dan hard-brakes before the water, shoulder strap taut, sees swirling wave-chop bright in the beams. Too deep? No depth post on this lanelet; couldn't be more'n a foot could it? Go through slowly or reverse a half-mile - lane too bank-narrow to turn round.

'Gonna go through slowly K. You snuggly-warm now?'

'Warm now Daddy. Can we have the Wiggles on?'

'Okay, but only if we both sing along, all right?' Dan switches to the CD player, unmutes the speakers and edges the car forward into the water. Too dark to see down for wheel depth even with lights dipped, but as they climb out again choppy red brake-lit wavecrests shine in the mirror.

'We made it, Katie!' As the guitar intro starts. The lane leads left and up, twists right under more swooping tree branches, then Dan brakes to stop again. A tree lies across the lane, ivy coverlet shiny, fluttering in the wet wind.

'Sorry Katie, got another problem.' Dan switches to full beam, peers past the sweeping untroubled wipers. Not a huge tree, but several leg-thick trunk stems. Could pull it clear? Enough to pass? Or reverse back through the surging dark stream? Might run a wheel off the submerged roadbed? Risky.

Jeff Wiggle's falsetto begins and Katie's high wavery voice starts too.
'Not singing Daddy! Come on.'
'Sorry Little K, Daddy's got to get out and see.' Pulling flappydamp coat back on. 'You sing. Back soon.'
Dan zips up, velcroes the hood tight, pulls on leather gloves and pushes his door open into the wind. Slips out. Slams and waves.

***

Katie sings You Make Me Feel Like Dancing all the way through, then an Australian song with a snake in it, before she wonders when Daddy is coming back. Still dark outside, with the fallen tree glistening clearly in the headlights. No Daddy in sight. Strong wind gusts shake the car, splatters of rain slap at her window. The Wiggles sing, drowning any small sounds from outside.

Katie sings along with a couple more songs. Everything's okay except for the horrible weather, and Daddy will be back soon, won't he? Another song and Daddy isn't back. Why not? She stops listening to the songs and thinks about Mummy. She's been away since Monday, and Daddy said she's coming home soon. Is it tomorrow or tonight? Not here now, anyway. Daddy's gone to move the tree in the road, but she can't see him anywhere in the lights. He's been gone quite a long time. The car seat straps hold her down, stop her from moving to see out properly. Can feel the engine still running but the car isn't moving - maybe she can get out of her seat? Never released the seat straps herself before, but seen Daddy and Mummy do it lots. Red button between her legs, but when she tries to click it, the whole strap-catch pushes down too. Has to get other hand under.. push together.. yes!

She pulls all the straps apart, arm-shrugs out, slips down onto the floor behind Daddy's seat, climbs across onto otherside back seat. Can get right up to window now, but muddy bank too close and dark to see much. Can climb to front? Katie squeezes between the seats, climbs over the black box lid that has CDs in, onto Mummy's seat. Glowing radio, Wiggles still singing, turns them down now. All the way to quiet, and other sounds come alive. Wind gust-whistle, rain-splatter, creaking trees with branch sway wind-toss. Quiet car engine purr, wiper slide-slap sometimes. Steady patter on car roof. Bird call... or was it a voice? Gone now.

Katie stands up on the seat, sees bright-lit tree branches still across road, reaches over for steering wheel, could climb to Daddy's side. She steps on knobby lever and whole car sudden-lurches, Katie thrown back between front seats. She screams - surprise not hurt. Pushes up again, pulls to front, engine not purring now, car still, lights gone dimmer. Hears small voice again. Daddy shout! Katie grips steering wheel, standing up, searches through windscreen between squeaky wiper swipes. There, through and under tree ivy, can see Daddy's leg, pale shoe sole... Daddy's there! Katie calls, shouts, loud in the car but maybe Daddy can't hear her. He's not coming, maybe stuck. Katie has to get out, go and see.

Coat! She has to get coat on first, for going outside. Over back, by car seat. Climbs through, finds arm hole, pushes in, pulls, makes hand come through. Can't find other arm hole, pulls coat round, tug and twist, can't bend arm in. There, done it now, pulls up sleeve. Tries zip. Too fiddly, can't do it. Squeezes past Katie seat, pulls door lever. Nothing happens, won't open. Must use Daddy's door. Climbs through seats, pulls past steering wheel, tugs door handle. Quite hard, pulls more. Yes. Door clicks, then flies open in wind gust, pulls Katie half out, but not quite tumbling down onto road. Light on inside car now, shining off wet road, rain spatters head, wind tugs at loose coat, now standing on dark wet road, tree fingers waving above.

'Daddy?' Katie trots through the rain towards the tree-tumble, crawls under the first trunk branch, getting wet from ivy and road, close to Dan's shoe. His head and shoulders are beyond the next trunk stem. She stands by his leg, peers through fluttering ivy. 'You okay Daddy?'

'Katie.' Weak voice, woozy. 'Hurt. Need help.'

Katie struggles over the wet bark further to the right, lower to the road. Car headlights pierce through patchily here, part of Dan's pale face, bright blood smear, trickle near his eye. Katie runs to crouch down and hug him, head on his chest. Dan is still, doesn't respond. Gusty wind still flaps the ivy leaves and blows Katie's blonde hair around, making her shiver as she sobs, reaching for Daddy's wet face, trying to get his attention. 'Daddy, wake up Daddy!'

Help for Daddy, must, no-one here. Phone! Daddy always has phone, where is it? Katie searches folds of wet coat, looking for pocket - finds it, but no phone. Climbs over Daddy, soft, wet, silent, tries other side. More blood here, coat sticky, but can feel phone in soggy-soft pocket. Won't come out, tangled in clammy wetness. Got it now... but no light, cracked and smashed, not working. What can she do?

Katie stands up, looks away from bright dazzle car lights. Rain eased to drizzle now and even a little light starting in the heavy sky, but Katie is scared, chilled and crying. Up the hill, further on, she thinks it's a long way to get anywhere. Behind her the car is dry, offers shelter, and she climbs back over the tree limbs, the slapping green leaves, runs into the blinding light. Katie stands at the open Daddy-door, looks up into dry safety, thinks of blood on cold pale skin. She slams the door, knows she must go through the ford for Charlie. Daddy would say no, and Mummy, but she has to paddle through the water. Get Charlie.

Light enough now to see little peaks of bubbles on the sleek-flow dark water, branches and leaves churning past, Katie stands, shoe toes touching the wavelets. Should have wellies, but they're at home. Might be deeper than wellies. Take shoes off? No. Sharp hurty bits maybe, unseen things. She knows it'll be cold; she's shivery wet now, but feet and legs will get icy. As the light grows stronger, shows the toss and dip of the branches, Katie steps into the waves. Just over her shoe, first step, and freezy water fills her left, gasps with the shock, but she steps in with her right, ankle deep. Iceblock cold, and now Katie feels the flood dragging at her feet, pulling her right. Can't stop, got to go through, get Charlie.

Katie steps on, three more steps and she struggles now, heavy ice-water pushing knee-deep from her left, dragging her rightwards. She stumbles, shrieks, waves her arms to balance against the water-force. Okay again, stands still, just numbing cold legs, shivery and scared, not sure she can fight the water-power. Memory flash of being knocked over by a seaside paddling-wave crash-breaking too close, knocking her down, salt drowny mouthful and soaked cardigan. Daddy can't pick her up here, pat and comfort her now.

Sees a stick charging towards her on the churn, thick and long, Katie grabs, slight kneebend only needed. Now she holds it, both hands, pushes against the underwater roadway on her right, fights the water-force. So cold, so afraid, but the stick's her friend, her helper. Two more halting stick-push steps and Katie can see she is halfway over, not far now. Reaches stick forward, pushes another slide-step. Once, twice, then the stick fold-snaps. Katie tips instantly into the urgent, careless water, right hand scraping rough concrete under the drowning ice-water waves pushing at her face, into her hair. Tumble-tossed, water-borne, mouth and nose filling, spinning, terror-grab finger-dash over freeze-slicked hard stones.

Then a nudge of softer something, grabbable hair, Katie clutches, holds, stops tumbling. If only she can hang on, get her head up. Out of the water, gasping, crying, struggling still she clings to her saviour, Yoda, Charlie's big hairy dog. Yoda drags sobbing ice-stunned Katie, her legs weakly pushing. Pulls her back through the flood, beneath dragged brambles and dangling branches, over slippery life-drowned river stones to the concrete roadbed. Charlie splashes in to meet them, lifts Katie, frozen wet child, shaking and coughing, water-snot spluttering.

'Daddy,' mutter-mumbles, 'help Daddy.'

'Katie, Katie! What on earth? Where's Dan?' Unzips his coat, 'Good boy, Yoda.'

Katie coughs, can't find words through shivers and sniffs, but waves onwards, over the ford, points. Charlie cuddles her closer, inside his coat flap now, treads carefully onward through the pushing angry waves, water climbing into big wellies, feet chilled like Katie. Trudges up onto road hardness, Yoda follows, round to the left, lighter now, enough to register cloud-dim of new rain threat. Up and right, Katie calmer, buried in Charlie's coat and there is Dan's red-tail car, lights still strong enough to help paint the tree toppled on Dan, shoe showing beneath.

'Bloody Hell!' Charlie strides forward to the car, peels Katie from his coat, onto the passenger seat, runs round to start the engine, neutral first. Takes off coat, returns to wrap Katie, comforts, tells her to rest, okay now, he'll go to Daddy. He does. Runs through re-starting raindrops, over the ivy to blanched, bashed Dan, pinned under rolled-over tree limbs, not moving. Charlie touches face, can't feel warmth, goes for pulse-check. Yes, but slight. Digs out his phone. Yoda noses Dan, watches Charlie.

'Yes, ambulance, right now, soon as you can! Yes, and firemen to shift the tree that's on top of him. What? Well, just whatever you can, quickly. Yes.'

Charlie pulls at the tree, but it's now settled heavy to its lowest rest, doesn't move. Calls again.

'Ted? Charlie, yeah. Look, an emergency Ted, it's bad. My neighbour Dan's under a fallen tree, out cold, above the ford in the lane. Fire service are all over the place, trees and floods, gonna be ages. Got your JCB handy? Get up here with chains? Soon as you can, boy. Okay?'

Back to the car, warmer inside, Katie sniffing, teeth still chattering, bundled on lonely front seat. Charlie climbs behind the wheel, backs and shunts the car tight to the hedgebank, further down from the tree. Rain beats heavier on the windows, still wild.

'Gonna get your Daddy out, Katie, make him safe. Mummy at home, is she?'

Katie shakes her head, sobs. They wait for help, Katie in the car, Charlie with his coat now wrapped over Dan.

***

Liz gets back, earlier flight, dashes home through puddled roads, full of fear. But now Katie is warm and dry, settled with Yoda at Charlie's, dressed strangely. Kisses, cuddles and tears. Tea, biscuits and comforting; pats and hugs for Yoda. Hospital visit soon; Dan is weak after surgery, but stable, safe.

Outside, still raining.

FRANGNAM WANNABEE MAN'S LUCKY DAY

Mike Moody

Jim sat playing his accordion in Framlingham market square. He did it twice a week and reactions were varied, a good number of people stopped for a minute, smiled and dropped a coin or two into his box. There were a few who frowned at him screwing their noses in distaste and others in a rush who just ignored him. Nobody was standing and listening for any length of time today – but occasionally they did stand, listen and appreciate his music and when they did he felt elated. The trouble was too many people were in a rush.

As he played his music words came into his head as they often did.

OK stare at me! - I'm no square - I'm sitting in a square so stare! - Then listen to me play - bootiful they say - both night and day - that's my way - they like the tune - they love the word - they wanna swoon - from what they heard.

I've seen this guy in a pop video called Gangnam Style, dancing round like a prat to rubbish music and he's famous! Well I'm better than him, I'm sure. Alright at this moment I am in this square in Framlingham, sitting and playing the piano accordion; the fact is I need to. But I am talented and just look at my dress sense: leathers (including cap) and shades, which reflect my cool composure. The pushbike and suitcase maybe let me down a bit, but of course I need something to get round on and protection for the accordion. But you've just got to focus on me and realise that when people appreciate my talent it will be Hit the Road Jim; probably on a Harley Roadster.

My music is real music, which I learnt in the army band. Now I'm a one-man band with this fantastic piano accordion. I might look a bit like the Gangnam Man, short and podgy, but I'm no star yet. Wish I was.

People love to hear me play the accordion in my own style and I'm sure they appreciate the cool look. So with their generosity I'll earn enough to get by; but for how long? I'm no star sat here, but feel I should be. I know I can do better than that guy on the video, and I will do whatever to become a star. All I need is for someone to believe in me and my talent and back me, because I do have talent and in the meantime? Well I'll keep going and see if I can make a few more pounds and perhaps have a drink at the bar at the Castle. What else can I do?

After packing up Jim walked up to the pub, which was not an easy task pushing the bike, loaded with suitcase and accordion, up the hill. He parked his bike and moved into the pub bar carrying his suitcase. After sitting in the sun and walking up the hill he was sweating and longing for a cold beer.

'How's it gone today Jim? Anyone spotted you?' George the barman always said that, and Jim gave him the usual grunt in reply. George smiled and responded, 'Well maybe tomorrow. The usual?'

'Yeah; but I tell you now I'll be ordering champagne when I hit the big time.'

'You want to try something different in your act. Why don't you try rap?'

'Don't think that - You silly prat - You taking the mick - You must be a dick - You know that rap - it's a load of crap - I got my style - Had it a while - Look at me - What do you see - A man who's cool - I'm no fool - Can't see it work - You style free jerk.'

'You got it!' laughed George.

'I know I've got it but, how do I get it out there? - It's no good in the square - It just ain't fair - They don't see I have flare - They just stand and stare. There I go again; you've really got me started on this rap thing. You were joking when you said try rap, but it's been going through my head for a while. Trouble is it's not music!'

Jim laughed.

Deep down Jim thought he wanted more than a gimmick that might bring success. He wrestled with the thought, do I care about success or the music I make? But not for long, Bollocks! I want success then I can do whatever. At the moment I'm a next to penniless piece of shit making a living on the streets. Give me success. Please God!

His thoughts were disturbed by George saying, 'You need a plan. You've been coming into this bar for over a year and making your meagre living off people's charity.'

'No way! I am being paid for my entertainment. If people didn't like the music I make they'd just walk by. I don't look like a beggar and I'm not. So get that straight!'

'OK. No offence Jim. But what are you going to do to move on with your life?'

'If I knew that I'd be doing it!'

'You need a USP just like that Gangnam man and then you need to get it on video and onto You Tube. Maybe try Britain's Got Talent'.

'You lost me on the USP.'

'Just business jargon Jim – Unique Selling Point. Like rap and accordion. I bet nobody's done that.'

'I wonder why?'

The bar started to fill up as people called in on their way back from work and George was kept busy pouring the drinks.

Jim was deep in thought wondering, how it had all come to this. He was getting by with his street performing and the odd jobs he did from time to time. He was living in something little more than an oval, a one-room apartment courtesy of social services.

Having left the army with his musical skills he thought he would be able to put them to use and earn a living doing something he loved. But he had slowly slipped down to the bottom layer of society in this small rural town. Perhaps he should have moved to the city, but he had been brought up in a village nearby and he knew a lot of people in the area were well off.

'Hey, wake up Jim,' George's voice brought him out of his daydreaming. 'I was just saying can I introduce you to this gent, but you didn't answer.'

Sorry George. 'Pleased to meet you Mister.'

'Just call me Adrian. George was telling me you're a street performer and are quite well known locally.'

'Well I guess so. Anybody walking through the market square on a sunny day is likely to know of me.'

'Can you show me what you do?'

Jim started to play his accordion; the usual stuff he played in the market square.

'No Jim! Give him some accordion rap, like you were doing earlier.'

'He doesn't want to hear that!'

'Sure I do!' Adrian piped up. 'Sounds unique to me.'

'OK then. Cover your ears!'

Jim started a melodic beat on his accordion and let the words flow…

'You think it's unique - the words you seek - you know the style - it's been round a while - but I am new - came out of the blue - doing my thing - singing my song - it has a nice ring - and rarely goes wrong…'

Jim continued for a little while then came to a close. 'And now my friend - the rap must end - so pay your due - say a pound or two.'

Adrian and George laughed, other people in the bar clapped.

'Jim you can go somewhere with that and I think I can help you.'

Jim's eyes lit up. 'You're joking!'

'No. I have connections in London, in the music and entertainment business.'

Would this be his chance? 'Tell me more'

Jim was asked to record some songs, which would be pushed around the music and entertainment scene. He did this and sent the results to Adrian, and every day since he had been on edge waiting for a message. Would it ever arrive?

FOUR YEARS OF ADVERSITY

Rosemarie Czarnocka

The invitation said: *Your attendance is required at the grand unveiling of The Arrival of the Performing Bear. Pickles and plonk provided. It was very tongue in cheek, and a little light hearted to celebrate the completion of her latest painting.*

Four Years earlier Rebecca had been commissioned to choose and copy one of two paintings from a Sotheby's catalogue for Robert, a friend of her husband Malcolm. One picture was titled The Two Suitors and the other The Arrival of the Performing Bear. She chose The two Suitors as there were only five people in the picture and she liked the story of a widow seated in a sparsely furnished room with her daughter and little boy, who was dressed as the matchmaker down to the walking stick and flower in his buttonhole. In the centre of the picture was an elderly gentleman whose gift to the woman was a pretty needlework basket. A younger man, who looked like a farmer, was leading a donkey foal in through the doorway, the door of which was hanging on one hinge.

Rebecca didn't like copying other artists' work, but there was nothing illegal about it so long as there was a label on the back stating "after……..", and the name of the original artist. Robert was delighted and paid handsomely for the painting. However, he remarked that he really would have preferred The Arrival of the Performing Bear and would she consider another commission for that one? Ever ready to accept a challenge, she agreed with some misgiving as there were forty five people in the picture and Robert wanted a large painting, oil on canvas, and the picture she would be copying was only 7" x 4".

The scene was that of a mid, nineteenth century east European village with straw roofed ramshackle cottages and fields and mountains in the background. Some of the villagers were on the rooftops to get a better view, young children were sitting, or standing round the edge of the village well and in the left foreground was a gypsy telling fortunes. At her side was a little boy sitting on a donkey. A large crowd was gathered round the central group of visitors in front of which stood the statuesque figure of the colourfully attired bear handler holding a chain which was attached to the collar of a great brown bear.

After printing out an A4 version of the photograph, squaring up both the canvas and picture she was copying, Rebecca spent a few months working on the background and constantly asking herself what on earth she could have been thinking taking on this difficult task and progress became spasmodic and very slow. On several occasions she found herself standing in front of the easel muttering "I hate you, oh, how I hate you."

She had other commitments being an active member of the village hall committee and she baked each week for the W.I. market. In addition Malcolm's health had been deteriorating for some time. He was becoming very forgetful and suffered lapses of memory sitting for hours in his armchair, sleeping or staring into space. He was unable to hold a conversation and sometimes didn't even appear to recognise his wife. He was diagnosed as having Dementia.

Work on the painting was held up for some time and after a while Rebecca decided she needed a short change of scenery and decided to visit her daughter, Sophie, in Leicester. She arranged for Malcolm to go into respite care for a few days, which he seemed to enjoy on a previous occasion.

The day before she was due to return home Sophie's mother-in-law invited them to tea. Rebecca disliked the mother-in-law who was very outspoken to the point of being extremely rude and she found it difficult to keep her tongue between her teeth. Rebecca and Sophie set off and turned into a road where cars were parked on both sides making it necessary to drive in the middle of the road. Suddenly a car emerged at speed from a side road and smashed into the front of Sophie's car. Rebecca felt a searing pain in her chest and was having difficulty breathing. Her daughter was convinced she was having a heart attack crying as she rummaged through her mother's handbag looking for her Angina pills. Meanwhile an onlooker had phoned for an ambulance and the Police arrived.

It was learned later that both cars were written off and the driver of the other vehicle had been drinking. Rebecca sustained a fractured sternum, several badly bruised ribs, and substantial soft tissue bruising. She was hospitalized for two weeks and spent a further eight weeks being pushed round Leicester in a wheelchair.

During the ten weeks she was in Leicester Rebecca had kept in touch with the care home regarding Malcolm's welfare, but the social workers, medical staff and family decided it was too much for her to continue looking after her husband and arrangements were made for him to remain in care.

On arriving home Rebecca felt guilty because Malcolm was in care and she missed him, all of which did little to motivate her to continue with the painting. She had spent two years on it so far and not very much had been accomplished. She began to receive phone calls as to when it was likely to be completed. After working a further twelve months on the painting she could see it coming together and only the forty-five people and foreground remained to complete the picture.

One afternoon as she was sitting in the garden enjoying the warm sunshine, she received a phone call from her elder daughter, Julie, who lived in Sheffield. After the usual, "Hello, how are you?" Julie said in a very subdued voice, "I'm sorry to have to tell you this Mum, but I've been diagnosed with cancer and the prognosis is not good." Rebecca let out a yelp and burst into sobs. It was such a shock.

There followed months of surgery and chemotherapy when Rebecca spend as much time as possible with Julie, especially when she was in hospital for a month undergoing what was known as the radical treatment. This involved bombarding the body with extreme doses of chemotherapy, removing healthy stem cells, transfusions, and replacing stem cells. It was heartbreaking for Rebecca sitting in the corner of her daughter's hospital room, listening to her teeth chattering and her whimpers of, "I'm so cold, Mum," and being unable to touch her. She had an extremely high temperature and Rebecca was aware of how seriously ill Julie was.

As a result of her positive attitude to her illness and a series of miracles, Julie gradually made progress and left hospital. Her breathing was difficult as she had lost the top half of her left lung, and there was further surgery, which made sure she would never be able to have children. In addition radiotherapy to the head had affected her ability to retain information in her memory and it was clear she never again be able to cope with a worthwhile occupation.

Eventually, after a lapse of almost a year, Rebecca found herself once again sitting at her easel with an apathetic attitude and even less motivation to complete the painting. It was not known at this point whether it would still be required as, unfortunately, Robert had died without ever seeing it. However, she made a pact that if she completed it by October (it was now the end of August) Julie would pull through and go into remission with the cancer.

At last the painting was finished after four long years of hard graft and adversity. Rebecca decided to have a few friends in and laid on a magnificent buffet to make it a special occasion. She made two short curtains from red velour, yellow cords, and tassels, fixed them to the easel, and sent out invitations. It was a light hearted and successful evening and next day she stood in front of the painting for the last time. There were so many things going on in the picture and each one held a story of its own.

She delivered the painting to Robert's wife who marveled at the detail and realistic likeness to the original, stating that her husband would have loved it and that she certainly wished to keep it.

Driving home Rebecca went over the past four years in her mind, remembering how much she disliked doing it and how difficult it proved to find the motivation to carry on. She realised the painting had gone forever and she felt an overwhelming sense of loss.

THE MONKEY PIPE

Will Ingrams

The call from Anya threw me totally. Into autopilot, while the brain reeled.

Replace telephone, wander back into kitchen, flick kettle on. Grumble and hiss of electrically heated water. Occupy boiling time rinsing mug, mind still stumbling, revive dining table laptop, remove last photo from scanner glass. Furious kettle roar simmers to quiet, tea bag time. Return to keyboard watching vapour hover above mug, lift, vanish like buried memories. Fingers move the mouse, find photo file scanned earlier. The head-held image.

Grandad Wilf in his old high-back chair straight camera-looking, defiant. My first picture, I think, framed in Box Brownie viewfinder window, waist-height breath-held steady. Memory glimpse of black knob twist, arrows to number eight exposure; generic recollection, perhaps. Photos, newspapers, television, inside comic pages - all black and white in those Billy Fury days. Real life had colour; oak green zip-up cardigan, yellow-stripe brown snake belt through fawn shorts. Grandad's pipe, deep tan, dark-scorched bowl-edge, black stem scarred paler by stained teeth. Zoomable today, can magnify smudgy hand on grainy chair arm, enlarged pipe indistinct, but not yet the monkey pipe, and Peter not born, not thought of.

Grandad Wilf spotted it first, afternoon-walking past local shops, tiny hand gripping rough-grained finger, paused under tobacconist's wound-out awning, there. Glass shelf propped, the monkey pipe, instantly captivating. Wondrous exotic, cheeky creature carved by imagined native hands under steamy-bright jungle leafshine, crouching hollow-tailed monkey proffers smoker's bowl; Grandad should tamp in wriggly-rich baccy, smoke, sigh. Wilf brought me up, feels like, though Mum and Dad were there too. Grandad was stern fun, wonder, adventure. We walked the high seas, slept in deserts, rode flying fishes, all before I started school. Doorbell jangled, but too late, monkey pipe just sold, nothing similar. Cross, dejected briefly, but memory-snagged, the monkey pipe.

Walking home, old enough, from Juniors, I wonder-spied it four years later, restored to window. Ran home, dragged Mum back - bolster meagre pocket money, surprise Grandad's sixty-fifth. Excitedly wrapped, fearfully given, opened and approval-smoked by twinkling Grandad. Peter was nappybaby then, too pink to include. Was always my Grandad monkey pipe, Nick's gift. Smell it now, impossibly, moist tobacco strands, sweet-puffed smoke. Only later the cold ash, the bitter residue.

Grandad fell while I was school-trapped. Hip smashed. He lay slumped, slept through growing years, no more world-walk adventures. Grumpy with pain, drug-sleepy, story-sharing seconds scarce. Smoking discouraged, Grandad still puffed the monkey pipe at times - maybe for me. Bedside waiting, dreamy book-looking hours, not unhappy. Peter never did. Trees, cowboys and cross-bows we shared, enjoyed, but not bedside time. Peter never walked wild with Wilf, Grandad never inspired Peter's life.

Back from Sheffield, college girlfriend homeshow weekend, visited Grandad final time. Nursing home less grim than many, no neglect-slap scandals then. Smiling nurse Joyce knew me well; Wilf had lingered long, hazy-vague, still Grandad. Dad visited father-in-law less once Mum died, consumed by cancer two years back, aching absence. Motherless teenager, Pete showed Anya the abbey as Wilf wheezed, muttered beside me. Awkward after - Anya distant, me unsettled. We split soon after, and Grandad died. Knew to expect it, seen the decline, but death hits hard. Finality.

The trust fund was for me, they said, and the monkey pipe; all else to Dad, Mum now gone. I hadn't known, expected. Nine hundred pounds was vast - a car, debts paid, a lusty Spanish summer. Peter wanted fair shares, angry and jealous. My Grandad though. Pete never visited the home, never cared. Never sucked the cold monkey pipe, smelt smoke, tasted tar.

Pete chucked Uni after a month, made sales, manager by twenty two. Christmas at doddery Dad's framed the row, cold turkey hangover. He started it.

'Old banger finally died then? Piece of crap you got with our Grandad money, eh?'

'Not our money, Peter. He left it to me.'

'Course he did. Always his sodding favourite, weren't you? Nicholas this and Nick bloody that. What'd you get up to with him, eh? Must've liked little boys, I reckon. Bit of fiddling, was it?'

'That's disgusting, Peter! How dare you say a thing like that about your own Grandad!'

'Well I don't know, do I? Never in on your little secrets was I? Hours in his bedroom, all I know.'

'You little shit! You never cared for him or for anybody else - except yourself, you sod!'

'Like you cared for him, you mean? Give him that creepy bloody pipe, so he could smoke himself to death? Get your money sooner, eh?'

I strode towards him, clenched to smash, but Dad peered in, puzzled by shouting, and I stormed out. Not spoken since, Peter and me. No words at Dad's funeral, not for our kids to be cousins. Grandchildren. Long years, gone so soon. Separate lives.

Tea mug cooler, no vapour, look up at the mantelpiece pipestand, grinning monkey still offers empty pipe bowl. Sweet. Bitter. Twenty minutes since that telephone call from Anya. Informed me of the accident, her Peter driving. Intensive care, touch and go. Didn't know if she should call. Would I want to know? Thanked her, no more.

Drink tea down. Close laptop, switch off scanner. Rinse mug. Return to phone. Retrieve last caller number.

ROUND THE BEND

Mike Moody

It was late autumn and as usual, when darkness fell early and the weather was inclement, fewer people were seen around the village of Brookstead. The only signs of life were lights shining from the windows of houses and the occasional car which passed through the village with headlights beaming. In the centre of the village houses were very old and the windows small. Through the window of the very oldest building six people could be seen sat around a table. Four men and two women, all well dressed and all with a large wine glass filled with a dark red wine set before them. The room was large but lit only by one lamp, a number of candles and a log fire. A passer-by giving a quick glance might think this was a cosy scene; a closer inspection would neither see nor hear laughter and despite the wine and apparent warmth the atmosphere in the room was distinctly cool.

A tall middle aged man with an intent expression was speaking to the others. 'The next full moon will be when it happens. You all understand what must be done and that it must be on sacred ground at sunset. We need a young woman to enable us to complete the task.'

Stephen looked into the faces of his followers. They were weak and needed his leadership; they were scared, it showed in the way their faces changed when he talked of sacrifice and a young woman. His followers were all of old families with roots in the land surrounding Brookstead. George and Jane were reliable. Keith was weak but would do as he was told. However Stephen was concerned about Julian's support. If Julian didn't support him then neither would Lauren. These two were the youngest in the group and most likely to rebel against his leadership.

Julian spoke up, 'You're asking a lot Stephen. So far sacrifice of animals has been sufficient; why take a human life this time? We'll be in deep shit if we get caught.'

'I'm not asking, I'm following the will of our Master. You have read the text in the Sacred Book of Beelzebub which has been passed down through the generations. The sacrifice of a young maiden whose blood adulterates sacred ground will ensure the continued protection of the coven and its growth. Also it takes us one step closer to eternal life in the service of the Master. We must follow the Master's will. If you are an unbeliever then leave.'

Julian stared Stephen in the eye, 'My family has been involved in this coven as long as anyone's. Do not call me an unbeliever. I am aware how our families have benefited by our membership and I have no intention of leaving. But if we pursue this action and it fails then we risk the very existence of the coven, not to mention our own freedom.'

'The only way of moving forward, of ensuring our survival, is to receive the blessing and support of our Master and in order to get it there must be a human sacrifice. However I say we put it to the vote and we will abide by the decision of the majority. Are we agreed?'

There was unanimous agreement and the vote took place. George, Jane and Keith supported the action; Julian and Lauren were against.

'We have four against two. The proposal is passed and we draw and mix our blood to bind us in this task.'

Each drew a knife across their hand and let their blood drip into the goblet held by Stephen. When each had shed blood into the goblet red wine was added to the mix. Stephen sipped first followed by the others.

'Now we must decide how we get our sacrificial maiden. George do I remember you saying that you could do with extra staff to assist with answering calls and admin work?'

'Yes. But I'm not sure we can afford it.'

'Why not advertise for a trainee receptionist/administration assistant. It should attract a number of young women. One could be picked for our purpose, another would be given the job. We will drug the drink of the chosen one. It must be one who has come to the interview under her own steam. We'll help pay the cost of keeping the trainee you take on for a while at least. Then if you can't afford to keep her you can get rid after six months.'

'I don't like the idea. If there is any evidence leading back to me I will be the suspect in the case of the missing girl.'

'Don't worry George I'll sort the detail with you and I'll join you as a friend helping in the interview. It might also help if a woman is there. Are you OK with that Jane?'

'I'm fine if George is.'

'Then the deed will be done much to the pleasure of our Master. I will sort out the details and liaise with each of you. We will go over them at our next meeting in four weeks time and the sacrifice will take place on the following Friday.'

The coven dispersed as Stephen saw them out into the dismal autumn night with the nearly full moon trying to shine through passing clouds. He locked the door and walked back into the dining room picking up the goblet which still held remnants of blood. He walked upstairs, entering a back room where a table stood with candles on either side and a small statuette of a demon in between. In front of the statuette was a clear glass dish filled with water. He bent over the dish, stared intently into the water and started to chant a prayer in the language of the coven and whilst doing this emptied the remnants of blood from the goblet. Then speaking in his own tongue, 'The coven will do your bidding Master and I seal this truth by giving you the blood of the coven. We will deliver your sacrifice after sunset at the next full moon.'

***

'Isn't this fantastic Nick, sitting in the garden on a warm autumnal morning listening to the birds singing? No traffic noise. And to be able to look at all the trees and plants, then have the pleasure of breathing clean air.'

A tractor rumbled along the country road which was beyond their back fence.

'You were saying?'

'I don't mind the odd tractor. It was the constant noise we heard at our last place that made the garden a place where we couldn't just sit and de-stress.'

'I know. It's great. No more driving through the outskirts of Brum with its constant traffic jams, hustle and noise. Best career move I ever made. I even enjoy driving to work along the country lanes with the radio on and very little traffic.'

'Don't I know it! You used to come home in a foul mood at times. Do you remember that last row when you were late back after being held up in traffic and dinner was spoilt?'

'Not likely to forget it. You blew your nut and I was dumbstruck. I'd never seen you go off like that. The day after I decided it was time to move on and I started looking for jobs elsewhere. It was a stroke of luck when I came across this job in Suffolk; the ideal place and a salary increase!'

'Living in Brookstead is a dream come true. The kids love their schools and don't have to be driven there and it only takes you fifteen minutes to get to work.'

'Yeah, and I'm relaxed when I get there. Then if I have a bad day at work the drive home relaxes me. Or usually that is; last Thursday I nearly hit a livestock lorry. He was going too fast round a bend and was partly on my side of the road. Good job I was going slow and hugging the nearside of the road. Fortunately that is a rare event.'

'Why don't we have a walk over to that old abbey you were talking about the other day? It will get the kids away from their computers and give us all a bit of exercise.'

'Grangefield Church you mean? Yes there are the remains of an abbey there. Like many it was dissolved in Henry VIII's reign and then used by the landowner for stone to build his house.'

'No need to show off just because you have a history degree.'

'I read it in that book I bought about the history of Brookstead. The history in this area is quite fascinating. Even this village....'

'Let's get ready. You can bore me and the kids while we're walking there. I'll get some sandwiches ready and we can have a picnic when we get there.'

David and Laura were dragged off their respective computers in spite of their protests, particularly from David, who was eleven and not "into" family outings. However once they were out in the sunshine and on the walk the moans dissolved and they enjoyed running on and exploring.

'What's that tower over there on the hill Dad?'

'That's where we're heading David. It's Grangefield church tower, one of the highest in Suffolk. You see the wall which surrounds most of it?'

'Yeah. A wall. So what?'

'Well that was originally the wall of an Abbey that once stood there. You know, where monks used to reside and do good deeds.'

'I've learnt about monks in history. Didn't they wear long hooded cloaks and do a lot of praying?'

'Sort of, it was a strict religious order which had a set of rule...'

'I'll just catch Laura up before she gets to that stile.'

Cath laughed.

'You'll never get them interested in history unless you put more adventure into it.'

'You're probably right.'

They reached the church and sat down by the wall for their picnic. Laura was staring at the high wall, apparently fascinated.

'What's over the wall dad? It must be high enough to be a prison.'

'I don't think so. More likely a graveyard.'

David piped up, 'Dare you to go in with me Lor.'

'I'm not scared..'

'Remember both of you it is not a playground. You can walk around and look but you mustn't be disrespectful. The ancestors of local people, maybe our neighbours, are buried there.'

The kids walked into the ancient graveyard with its old family tombs and headstones, worn by the weather and covered in lichen. The graveyard was for the most part enclosed by the high wall which had been part of the abbey. The kids' eyes lit up when they saw depictions of skulls on some tombs.

'There are skeletons under these stones Lor. Don't stand near a grave or they might reach and grab your ankle. Then you'll be pulled into the ground where they will pull you apart and eat you.'

'Don't be silly. I don't believe you.'

She turned to walk away and David dropped on one knee in the long grass shouting, 'Help Lor. I stood too close. Help!'

She turned and looked at her brother with only one leg showing. She ran and screamed, 'Daddy!'

David jumped up and ran after her, 'I'm only kidding Lor. Stop running.'

They both stopped, seeing their mum and dad walking through the gate to the graveyard.

'I thought we said no running. And stop frightening Laura, you'll give her nightmares.'

'I'm not really scared mum. Anyway there are no such things as ghosts.'

'Too right. My clever girl,' Nick laughed.

The family had a look at the church and then walked back across the fields sticking to the footpaths. As they got nearer to Brookstead they saw a man heading towards them with a shotgun held under his arm. As he got near Nick greeted him, 'Hello there, are you out to shoot rabbits?'

'What's it to do with you? Make sure you keep your kids on the path. This is my land and I don't want outsiders ruining my crop.'

'Charming, and I thought this village was really friendly,' Cath remarked after the farmer had passed by.

'Don't worry about one bad apple. Most people we have met have been very friendly and the neighbours are great. In fact when I get back I'll see if Graham knows anything about that guy.'

When they got back they saw Graham in the front garden and told him about their encounter.

'It was probably Stephen Brooke, one of the large landowners round here. Thinks he owns the village! There are a few of them and some are a bit a cliquey and don't like newcomers in the village. Some of them have families going back centuries so I guess they are reluctant to change and are resentful of rights of way across their land. Fact is their influence in the village is dwindling. They always used to get what they wanted, but with the influx of people from East London and Essex over the last twenty years it's not so easy for them.'

***

Deborah had driven from Leystone on her scooter. It had been a pleasant drive, but as she parked it she felt nervous. She really wanted a decent permanent job and this could be the one.

She walked into the reception area.

'Hello. I'm Deborah Canning, here for the interview for the position of secretarial/administration assistant.'

'Very pleased to meet you Deborah. I'm Jane. I'll take you through to Stephen and George who'll be doing most of the interviewing. Don't look so nervous, we're a small friendly business.'

Jane knocked on the door of the nearest office.

'Come in. Come in,' shouted a voice from the other side of the door.

'Gentlemen this is Deborah.'

'Come in Deborah and please take a seat. I'm George Saxstead and this is Stephen Brooke. Jane will be joining us in the interview as she knows most about the job.'

Deborah sat upright on the chair trying her best to look confident, but thinking, *Thank God Jane is here. I don't like the look of these two middle age guys with grins all over their faces.*

George started the interview, 'I can see from your CV that you have not long left school with good A Levels but have just been working in waitressing jobs. Tell us what interested you about this job.'

'I really want a job that offers me a sound future. I'd like to work my way up in a business, but realise I must start at the bottom and learn the ropes. I will have to be trained but I learn quickly and will put every effort in to make a success of the job.'

She noticed that the guy called Stephen was looking her up and down whilst George started to explain what the Company did in some detail. *Old letch*, she thought.

Stephen butted in, 'So do you live with your parents Deborah?'

'No. I left home to live with a friend. We share a flat in Leystone.'

'Oh! Is that your boyfriend?'

'No,' she said, thinking, *None of your f...ing business.*

'And how did you get here?'

'I have a motor scooter.'

'Oh! Very good.'

That was the clincher. Stephen turned to George and smiled. A shiver went up Deborah's spine.

'Well thank you for letting us know something about you. Perhaps Jane can get you a drink and we'll chat about the job and your suitability for it.'

George gave a few more details about the company whilst Jane brought the drinks through.

'There's your tea Deborah, just one spoon of sugar?'

'Please.'

Deborah finished her tea whilst listening to Jane giving her details of the work she would have to do. After talking for about ten minutes she asked, 'Is there anything else you would like to know?'

'What hours will I work?'

Is that the best I can do, she thought as she tried to listen to what Jane was saying. But it all sounded distant. She looked at Stephen and George. Their smiles seemed bigger.

Jane stopped talking and there was silence for a little while.

'Anything else you would like know dear?'

Deborah's drooping eyelids rose, "And wor … abow the pay rai … sss"

Deborah's head flopped. She felt limp but could hear talking.

'She's out for the count. Jane, you prepare her for the ceremony. Remove her makeup and dress her in the ceremonial white robe. George and I will hide the scooter and incinerate her clothes and personal belongings. Keith, Julian and Lauren will join us here after five thirty when everyone else has left. We'll put her into the back of their estate car and drive up to Grangefield graveyard.'

***

It was Friday, Nick had been able to leave work earlier than usual and was driving back home. The sun was setting, its bright light dazzling him as he drove along the winding country lane that took him back home. He usually drove at a fair speed on the quiet roads, but on this occasion he eased off the accelerator thinking it was best to go a little slower when you can't see what's coming round a bend. As he turned the corner the sun moved to his right and as it did he saw a dark figure emerge in front of him. He slammed on his brakes and the car skidded to a stop. The engine cut out. There was no thud and no sign of the figure in front. He looked to his right on the other side of the road. There was nothing, no people, no cars, no animals and everything was still.

He wondered whether he had really seen anything and quickly came to the conclusion that it must have been a trick of the light, even though it had seemed so real. It was dangerous to remain where he was, parked on a sharp bend, so he turned the ignition, but nothing happened.

'Sod it!'

He tried again; nothing. A surge of panic went through him as he thought of someone hitting him from behind; especially if it was one of those livestock lorries which he saw daily, driving too fast on the narrow roads. He shivered as he thought about it; he wouldn't stand a chance.

'Keep calm, keep calm. Hazard warning lights on. Get out of the car and call recovery service from your mobile.'

He got out of the car and could neither see nor hear any traffic. Moving across the road to the safety of a grass verge he dialled the recovery service.

'Damn, of all the times to lose a signal.'

He decided to walk to the next village which was on higher ground where he could get help from residents if his signal didn't return on the way there. Leaving the car with a warning triangle placed some fifty yards behind it he started to walk.

The sun had just about set, it was very dim and would soon be dark and he thought it best to increase his pace. Then from the corner of his eye he saw a figure move in the field next to the car.

'Hello. Hello!' he shouted, whilst waving his arms hoping to catch the person's attention.

No answer came from the figure, which just kept moving slowly away from the scene without looking back. The stark silence was then broken by the hoot of an owl. Nick stared at the scene in front of him; a cloudless still night with no movement other than that of the figure in the field. He wondered whether to ignore the figure and stay on the road but decided to run after him. All he wanted was a little help.

By the time he found a reasonable gap in the hedge the figure was about four hundred yards away walking steadily up the hill. The field was muddy after recent rain and the clay soil stuck to his shoes making the pursuit very difficult. The figure was wearing a long coat or robe and kept a regular pace, almost like it was floating across the field. It just struck him that he could see no legs. Why hadn't he noticed that before? Then he realized he had. The shadow he had seen in front of the car had no legs just a long robe that touched the floor. Was it a woman? What would a woman in a long robe be doing walking across a field on a late winter's afternoon?

He couldn't make any sense of what he was doing. It was like he was being dragged by a will which he couldn't resist. He didn't want to resist, he wanted to find out where the figure was going and he was slowly catching up despite the mud which was weighing heavy on his shoes. The problem of the car had completely left his mind. One thought consumed him, *where was the figure going and why had it ignored him?* "It" not he or she was how he now felt about the figure. He was sure he was being encouraged to follow, at one point he would seem to be getting closer, but when he next looked up he was further away.

A full moon was rising in the clear sky and as daylight dwindled moonlight became a good substitute and he was able to continue his pursuit. The figure was heading for the parish church at the top of the hill which he recognised as Grangefield Church. The church tower stood tall, a dark shadow in the bright moonlight, dominating its surroundings.

He remembered that there were some cottages not far from the church. Should he make for them rather than keep following the figure? It was common sense, but he couldn't do it, something wasn't right, he could feel it in his bones. He wondered what the hell he was doing here yet he continued to walk on.

The mysterious figure reached the boundary of the churchyard and seemed to disappear through the high wall. Nick reached the wall but not where the entrance was. For the first time he thought of the figure as ghostly yet at the same trying to work out some logical explanation for the disappearance. It must have climbed over when he wasn't paying attention. What was waiting behind the wall? He broke into a cold sweat and a shiver went down his spine. Wanting to break the silence and tension he said in a low voice, 'This is getting seriously spooky!' Then much louder, 'Hello! Is anyone there?'

No reply. The silence was stark, all pervading and menacing, as if something was waiting for him beyond the wall. Nevertheless he was still drawn on and started to climb. As he pulled himself up he could see over into the graveyard where there was a glimmer of light just across from the church tower. He slid himself over, landed and turned to face the light. He wasn't sure but he thought he could see the back of the person or thing he had been following. It was standing still by a large chest tomb and the light he had seen came from the large candle that it was holding. Nick edged forward warily, looking from side to side. The shape remained still, its appearance becoming clearer as he got closer. He could now see that the robe was that of a monk, the hood covered the head and the dark robe was belted with rope. He wasn't sure what he should do, he was breaking out into a cold sweat as the scene was so unreal. But then with a tremor in his voice he blurted out, 'Hello! What are you doing? I nearly knocked you down back there on the road. What were you doing walking on that road and why didn't you answer when I shouted?' What was he saying? It was ridiculous, but he was eager to break the silence.

As his voice faded the silence seemed to be heavier. The monk stood perfectly still. He could see what he thought were pale legs to one side of the monk, on top of the tomb. Probably a carved figure, but he wasn't sure in the moonlight. They looked very pale, lit up in the white light of the moon whilst the tomb itself was grey and scarred with time. The more he stared the more he became convinced they were human legs.

He stopped in his tracks and pulled out his mobile phone and found he had a signal; it gave him some comfort and a little confidence.

'Is that a body on top of the tomb?' he said shakily.

The monk beckoned him forward with a slow movement of his arm. Nick moved towards the monk, mobile phone in hand. The monk stood taller than Nick and appeared to grow as he got nearer and as it did its body began to fade and Nick could see the body of a girl dressed in a white robe lying on top of the chest tomb. Now focussed on the girl he moved forward walking through the fading shape that had been the monk and saw that the girl was drawing breath with difficulty. She was unconscious and blood was seeping from a deep cut on her lower right arm onto the tomb, where a pool had gathered and was dripping over the side. But she was still alive and he needed to get help.

Nick quickly rang 999 and was put immediately in touch with emergency services.

He blurted out, 'I'm with a girl who's unconscious and bleeding badly from a cut on her arm. I'm in Grangefield Church yard just outside the village.'

'OK. Just keep calm. An ambulance and police assistance will be despatched. They should be with you soon. We'll stay on the line and give you instructions what to do. Do you have anything to tie around her arm to ease the blood flow?'

'Yes I have a tie.'

He took it off and tied it around the girl's upper arm.

'OK. That's done. What do I do next?'

He couldn't hear what they said, the signal was breaking up.

'I can't hear you!' he shouted anxiously

'…raise…..lessen..'

'Repeat! Repeat! You're not coming through clearly.'

He knew he must keep calm, but was finding it difficult and despite the cold night air was breaking into a sweat as his heart pounded.

The signal became stronger and clear as the instructions came through again.

'Raise the girls arm and apply pressure with your other hand to reduce blood flow to the wound.'

He noticed bruising on her arm, like she had been held tight, yet there was no bump or cut on her head so what had caused her to become unconscious?

'Now just keep the arm like that until the paramedics arrive. I will stay on the line until they arrive. Just let me know if there is any change in the girl's circumstances.'

Time seemed to slow and he hoped and prayed that an ambulance would arrive soon before she lost too much blood. As he stood shivering, his body damp with sweat, he could not see any sharp objects near the tomb. It didn't look like the girl had tried to commit suicide. However he could see that the grass around the tomb and back to the church path had been trampled by several people. What had they been up to and why had they fled leaving the girl's body there?

As he stood there he felt a friendly presence which had a calming effect. The ghostly monk reappeared and as it did images flashed through his mind. An Abbot and monks praying for the last time at the Abbey, praying that their brethren buried in its sacred grounds would maintain its sanctity forever more. Then soldiers dispersing the monks, making them leave the Abbey.

A more modern picture then came into his mind, four men and three women, one being the young girl on the tomb. They were walking through a car park with just two cars parked; the girl was unconscious and being held up by two of the men and being dragged along. They came to an estate car opened the rear door and bundled the girl into the back.

'Keith, Julian and Lauren take this car to Grangefield church. I'll take George and Jane in my car and meet you with the gear. We should be in place by sunset.'

'Can we be sure there will be no one there?'

'Julian it's autumn, a week day and early evening. It's very unlikely there will be anyone there. If we see signs of anyone then we'll drive past.'

Next Nick saw the two cars arrive at the churchyard. It was empty. The one who had been giving orders got out of his car and quickly looked round, then instructed the other driver to check round the churchyard.

'All's clear.'

'OK. Julian, you and Keith get her out and take her to the chest tomb by the tower. Be sharp about it as the ceremony must begin as darkness starts to fall. The rest of us will bring the gear.'

The girl, still unconscious, was lifted from the car and carried to the chest tomb on which she now laid.

Six people stood around the tomb all wearing dark robes, with hoods and chanting. The leader spoke but the elder woman held a long sharp knife.

'For you Dark Lord we spill this blood on sacred ground and swear to be your servants forever. In return we ask your help in pursuing our earthly goals and to bring us closer to eternal life in your service.' The woman holding the knife drew it slowly across the arm of the unconscious girl on the tomb. As the first blood was shed and drops hit the ground the breeze in the air grew into a wind and the branches of the trees swayed and they shed the few remaining leaves. The dim light following sunset seemed to grow darker and several tombstones fell.

'What the hell is happening?'

'Shut up Julian, I must finish the ceremony. There must be more blood and then the final words are to be spoken.'

As the woman made a move to make another incision there was a loud crack and the earth appeared to move.

She dropped the knife, screamed and pointed, 'Look! Skulls!'

The others lifted their heads and looked where she was pointing.

All around skulls were rising through the earth, with cloaked bodies following, bony hands stretched out. It was all happening quickly; dozens of skeletal monks were rising from their burial place and heading for the tomb where the young girl lay. The women screamed and fled down the nearby path to the cars with the men following quickly behind.

As they fled a further ghostly monk came through the surrounding wall, exactly at the spot Nick had seen it enter not long before.

The noise of a siren brought him back to the real world. The ghostly monk was no longer there.

The girl was still alive and he had eased the blood flow. She was going to live! The sole spectre or the group of long dead monks must have scared off the people performing the ritual and willed him from his car to save the girl.

Then the silence was broken by a loud crash down in the valley where the road was, and his car. His immediate thought was that the ambulance had hit his car.

'Oh no! Oh shit. What now?'

He broke into a sweat, scared that the poor unconscious girl would die on him. There would not be time to get another ambulance to her.

On the phone someone was saying, 'What is it. Explain what has happened. Keep calm.'

Then up above he heard a whirring noise which was getting closer and then he saw lights. Unable to get his head around what was happening he just looked up mesmerised by the bright lights. The whirring became a roar and the lights descended and he could clearly see the shape of a helicopter lowering itself in the field next to the church. On its side in bright luminescent yellow was the sign Air Ambulance. A smile of relief came to his face.

In to his phone he bellowed, 'It's the air ambulance.'

He turned to the girl on the tomb, a big smile on his face.

'You're going to live girl. The air ambulance is here!'

***

Back in Brookstead six people sat around a table. There were arguments going on.

'Silence! The deed has not been completed. Her blood was shed but not her life blood. We must try again.'

'Are you crazy Stephen? The girl knows the identity of you, George and Jane.'

'Julian keep calm, the potion she was given will eliminate any memory the girl has of that day. Only George, Jane and I knew of her presence and if anyone asks she never turned up.'

FIRE

D. Green

So fierce was the heat from the fire's glowing depths, that the wall of the egg nestled within, became semi-transparent, and Rhone looked out on hell.

Upright creatures that walked on two limbs, circled the pit, peering down through bulbous glassy eyes, which reflected the fiery flames from below.

Rhone hunched tightly into himself, as a tap then another tap echoed and shivered against his egg's outer casing, the last defence against them - the enemy.

He let a puff of breath out, expanding his chest. The steam settled and hardened on the inner wall blocking out the hated black shadows of the enemy above.

Vision gone but sound ever present, there was no mistaking the crack of a shell to Rhone's left and the shrill shout from an Upright. Then those terrible sounds of his brother Slate's shell being tapped away, the egg disintegrating, screams of outrage, sounds of chains rattling, and heavy dragging.

He had seen it so many times before. He refused to watch through the patches of transparency, just listened to the meaningless gibberish from the Uprights as they dragged his brother from the pit into slavery.

Day after day, week after week, Rhone defied the tapping probes of the Uprights. Daily he grew stronger, his body hardening, the fragile bones turning into bone-hard weapons. The steam of his breath no longer whispers of vapour to harden the inner shell, but flickers of flame to match the fierce glow within the pit.

He was their Chosen.

In the darkness of the night their whisperings reached him, their sadness, their shame at being forced to do terrible deeds. Their grief for the mutilated.

He was their last hope.

He would not fail them.

It would be this night. All day he had drawn air deep inside the cavity of his chest. He could no longer see through the blackened shell. The Uprights thought it lifeless, they were wrong.

One strike he would have, one strike would be enough.

The others had watched and planned carefully.

He must be silent. Surprise was a weapon.

One swipe of his leathery snout shattered the wall of his safe harbour, both heavily taloned feet crushing the blackened eggshell to dust.

He unfurled his wings testing their strength, once, twice, he flailed at the fiery flames, and rose from the pit as a fire spun warrior, bright and glowing, trailing fire and molten lava over the city below.

One long breath of fire to the left incinerated his brothers and sisters kept as pets and lab animals, their wings clipped, their fire sacs cut away. Their cry of thanks echoed through his mind.

Twice he cast across the city beneath him, watching as buildings shattered and melted beneath the onslaught of his fire, and then he turned his gaze towards the sliver of orange light on the far horizon, and sent out a mighty roar of defiance.

A clarion call to invoke Dragon Lore, one free, all free.

He flew on and on towards the orange orb in the sky, once looking over his shoulder to see many winged shadows following in his path to freedom.

Welcome, acknowledged the shiny orb to its kin born of fire, now to become its new children.

Raging heat choked his lungs, blinding light seared his eyeballs; flames crisped his wings and dissolved his bones.

Destruction to be reborn again in freedom.

Victory.

THE TABBY CAT

Anne F. Clarke

At night the wild warrior hunts.
Her world is full of scent messages.
She threads her way through tall spiky grasses.
Seed head bombs burst when she steps on them.

Tall saplings like skyscrapers reach
High into the dark blue velvet sky.
They are lit by the lamp of the yellow moon,
Whilst black shadows populate the village of the great wood.

She is fearless in her quest for prey.
Rabbits, voles and mice living amongst
The mossy cushions of the woodland floor
Have little chance of survival against her supple ferocity.

Yet in the light of day she is compliant.
When asked, she is a soft, stripy pillow
Comforting a child with earache,
Leaning its head against her mewling, murmuring body.

Her other life in the darkness of the wild wood forgotten until tomorrow's hunting.

DOMESTIC BEASTS

Will Ingrams

'I didn't call you catty.'
  'Oh really?'
  'No. I said you were cat-like - entirely different. It's a good thing.'
  'So I'm selfish, spiteful and manipulative, and it's a good thing.'
  'No. That's a complete misunderstanding on at least two levels. You're reacting to the word *catty* - which I didn't use - and its connotations, but that word has nothing to do with cats. Cats aren't selfish or spiteful - that's anthropomorphism. They just behave in a way that works for them in their world. Look - they like food and get it the easiest way they can, they luxuriate in warmth and comfort and they don't have a well-developed pack instinct, like dogs. I was just saying that you remind me, in some ways, of a cat.' Luke chunked his pint glass down on the weathered table plank and grinned, peace and understanding restored, hopefully.
  'Bollocks. A cat will puncture your leg through your jeans, just to get comfortable, it'll torture a mouse to death, slowly and cruelly, and then try to sit on the person that wants it least. That's how you see me, is it?' Head toss, unmollified.
  'God Lisa, give me a break will you? I like you. I think I love you a little bit, already. I know I love it when you snuggle up to me, relaxed and content. I was just trying to be perceptive. And nice, actually.'
  'Were you really, Luke? Now you're like an dirty dog trying to get his end away!'
  'Yeah, and I'm in the doghouse wthout a bone. I'll leave now, shall I?'
  'No, you won't. You'll follow me home, just as long as you're ready to stroke me really nicely when we get there. Make me purr. Maybe we can try finding your bone.'
  'Woof.'

PERFECT

D. Green

'Hello.' I looked up from my sweeping into several smiling faces.

'You said you would like to meet our ponies,' grinned Philip, the local squire's son. Philip was in my class at my new school. He had taken me to our local cinema last week to watch Black Beauty. I felt my cheeks redden remembering how he had held my hand throughout the film, and his goodnight kiss had been a dream, my first. Did I have a crush on him, oh yes, a bad one.

'Oh yes please.' I opened the yard gate and seven riders filed into the courtyard and dismounted. I saw my mother look quickly out of the kitchen window.

I met the older children a month ago, when I joined my new school.

'I know I've said this before but you are so lucky to be able to ride straight out into the forest,' Philip said with a smile and turned to his twin sisters. 'Girls, this is Alex.' Philip suddenly looked a bit shy. 'Emma is the one in green ribbons on the brown and white Shetland, he's Butterball.'

I patted the small pony and asked his small pig-tailed rider how old he was.

'Butters is ten.' She flung her arms about the shaggy neck. 'He's the best pole pony in the district,' she declared proudly and then added, 'I'm six.' She lent forward and whispered, 'Philip keeps talking about you at home.' Philip gave me a wink and kept on with his introductions.

'Rose has red ribbons, and this is Reggie, he's a New Forest and a dab hand at gymkhana games.' Rose gave me a shy smile and I patted Reggie's brown nose.

'You've met Jack.' Philip laid his hand on the neck of the black horse. 'This is Jasper, he's Irish bred and a whiz across country.'

I smiled at sandy haired Jack and patted tall, black Jasper.

'I'm Amy,' said a girl with fair curly hair. 'This is Moon; she's a Connemara from Ireland. She's brilliant in tack and turnout and family pony classes.'

I stood back and admired the snow-white pony. 'She's very handsome, how do you keep her so clean?'

'Endless washing, I get through bottles of shampoo, mum's always moaning about the cost.'

Philip turned to two boys who I hadn't met before. 'Larry and Paul have just come back from visiting their aunt in Scotland, their mum owns the village grocery and bakery and their dad is our local blacksmith.'

Beneath the brothers' riding hats wisps of light blonde hair stuck out.

'I'm Paul,' said the older brother. 'I'm in the same class as Jack and this is Rollo. He's a Connemara like Amy's pony and we sometimes do the pairs class and musical ride.'

'Such a pretty colour, dun isn't it?' Time to let them know I had some knowledge even if I didn't have my own pony.

'That's right and Larry's pony, Mouse, is a Highland, but a dark dun. He belongs to my aunt in Scotland but her girls are away at college, so she let Larry have him for as long as he wants. He's rock steady and looks after you well doesn't he?' He glanced across at his younger brother.

'He's the best,' confirmed Larry with a grin, patting the stocky pony.

Paul quietly said in my ear. 'Larry had a bad accident last year, a new pony bolted with him and smashed his leg on a tree. Off school for three months and still limps a bit now but he's fine on Mouse.'

'And finally,' Philip turned to his dark bay cob standing patiently, with his lower lip drooping, 'this is Donald. Dad wanted me to get something with a bit more thoroughbred in it, until I led the whole hunt over the stone wall at Thatcher Creek last winter, never puts a foot wrong out hunting. Mr Reliable aren't you mate, especially for taking the girls out.' He slipped a polo from his pocket and Donald gently took it from the palm of his hand. 'He'll be perfect for them when they get taller.'

I patted Donald's silky fur neck.

'So when are you getting a pony?' Amy asked.

'Dad says next year. I'm to work at Mrs Davies through the summer holidays to learn about horse care and tack and, if I'm still keen after the winter then I can have my own pony next Spring.' I shrugged. 'A while to wait yet, but at least I'll be riding more than when we were in London. It was just once a week there and mainly indoors with the occasional hack around the park, so to ride across those hills and forests is going to be a real adventure for me.'

They all laughed and Larry said, 'That is exactly what we call our days out, adventure days. We take a pack lunch and go right up to the top of

Glendale, you can see for miles, or go through the forest to Hallett's Waterfall.'

'Children,' said my mother. 'Lemonade and cakes.' I beamed my thanks to my mother as she placed a tray laden with glasses, a pitcher of lemonade and plates of biscuits and cakes on the courtyard wall.

'Mrs Harding, would it be alright for Alex to come to the woods with us on her bike?' Philip passed a plate of cupcakes to Jack. 'We're going to put up a few jumps and then take the girls up to the lower meadow so they can practice cantering.'

'Won't it be too steep for a bike?' Mrs Harding looked up at the surrounding hills.

'Alex can leave her bike at the warden's cottage, and then we can take turns walking and riding up to the meadow.'

'Riding.' I heard myself squeak.

'Well as long as you all keep a close eye on her. Alex isn't so used to being around ponies like you are. You need to change into your jods dear, and don't forget your hat.'

So I spent an idyllic summer holiday of adventure days and sharing ponies, and spent as much time up at the Hall, Philip's home, as I did my own. The monthly horse shows were a highlight and I cheerfully supported Upper Valley Blue Team (us) who unfortunately, only achieved second or third placing overall never getting quite enough points in the dressage.

At Mrs Davies small riding school and livery yard, I learned stable management and was overjoyed to learn from my instructors, that I had good stick ability and natural balance.

'So who is your favourite pony at the riding school?' asked Amy one evening when I was helping her wash Moon's mane and tail.

I didn't hesitate. 'Oh, Gem. He's a real friend and such a smashing colour. Like a dark conker and he has a more chocolate coloured mane and tail, but it tends to go bushy.'

'If you plait them they will start to lie flat and get easier to groom. Moon's used to be just like that.'

'I don't have time to do that, Mrs Davies likes all the ponies brushed off in the mornings, then last thing at night before they go out in the field.'

'It will be so much better when you get your own pony, you can groom all you like then.'

'Yes, but I won't have time to help you with Moon,' I teased and Amy laughed.

'Hi, girls.'

I turned round and gave a cry of delight, running over to Philip and giving him a hug, which he returned with a laugh, saying, 'Don't you get shampoo all over me.'

Amy rolled her eyes and sighed, 'You two.'

'Philip, Mrs Davies says I can move up from the riding school ponies and see how I get on exercising some of the livery ponies, what do you think?'

Surprisingly, Philip frowned. 'Well I'm pleased for you of course. Your riding has improved so much since you moved here.'

'That's because our ponies are so good,' cut in Amy smugly.

'The thing is Alex, just be careful you don't get put upon by some of the livery owners because they are too nervous to get on themselves. I'd hate to see you hurt and lose your confidence.' Philip took both my hands and squeezed them.

'You two are always smooching. Paul says it's young love. I think it's gross.' We both laughed at her.

My first livery pony to take over exercising was Prince. Aptly named and admired for his dark chestnut coat and flaxen mane and tail. At this moment though I was calling him less complimentary names as he sidled and swung his quarters into the traffic. Using my heels, I finally managed to kick him up the inside of Gem, who was placidly walking towards the forest entrance taking not the slightest notice of the few cars crawling pass the string of ten ponies.

Gem's rider looked across at me, his eyes wide, as he watched the antics of Prince now cantering practically on the spot.

'Gosh, he's naughty, glad I'm not on him.'

Then there was King with his satin black coat and not one white hair. An easy ride until winter came and mud appeared, then he turned into a demon, and liked nothing better than to collapse at the knees and roll in the deepest, wettest mud he could find. Not just one side of course but right over, plastering the saddle in thick slimy mud which then had to be sat on to ride home.

Neither whip, nor spur, kept him upright and you had to be quick to get off when he went down, or risk a crushed leg. Cantering in endless circles I found did the trick, while gates were negotiated, and I would be the last rider through, spraying mud and water as I desperately tried to keep him moving.

Finally, there was Jet who lived up to his name. 0-60, the moment his feet touched grass, iron mouthed, you had to grapple with him in a double bridle.

All through the winter months I rode those three, even managing to get Prince to walk a straight line through traffic, unless a bus came and he would canter on the spot.

One wet morning, mounted on Jet, the reins became so slippery that he got away from me. The feel of those bunched muscles lowering and thrusting forwards would have been exhilarating on another pony, but this was Jet, and he was running wild straight towards a four foot row of thorn bushes and behind those I could see a fence rail.

Even with both hands hauling on one rein, there was no turning him and I felt him gather himself to attempt to jump the whole. I remembered thinking, do I jump off or stay with him, but the decision was taken from my hands when a woman walking her dog and holding a huge umbrella walked round the corner. Jet took one look and spun sending me flying over his shoulder, across the thorn bushes to crash into the fence railing, my right arm taking the full brunt of the impact.

I vaguely remember the woman snapping shut the umbrella and running over to me saying, 'What have I done? Did the umbrella frighten him? I'm so sorry.'

Hastily I assured her that I was thankful she had appeared, or a far worse accident could have happened. Obediently I moved my legs and good arm to check nothing was broken and she helped me to my feet. By now the rain was relentless and we were both soaked through.

'I'll take you to my car and down to the village hospital.'

'Thank you, but I need to help get the ponies back to the yard. See,' I wiggled the fingers and wrist of my numb arm, "nothing broken just bruised. Would you mind calling into Seagull Cottage and asking my mother to collect me from the riding school?'

'Oh, you're Olivia Harding's daughter. I'll go now.'

I scrambled back through the undergrowth; my bad arm shoved into my jacket and went in search of Jet.

Halfway across the field there was a shout and Pippa, one of the instructors, came trotting towards me riding Gem and leading Jet. 'What a brute, I had just turned the ride to head home and I saw him bolt, what a wicked creature. Oh, you've hurt your arm. Do you think you could manage to ride Gem back to the yard and I'll ride this monster, I'm double your weight which will serve him right.'

The first person I saw, as our bedraggled group entered the stable yard was my mother standing in her long mack, white faced and tight lipped. As soon as my feet touched the ground she bundled me into our car, never giving me time to thank Gem for bringing me safely home.

Twenty stitches later, and an overnight stay in the village hospital, I returned home only to develop a shocking cold, which kept me red nosed and in bed for a week. It wasn't until ten days later on a Saturday morning that Philip and the others were allowed to visit.

'Poor you. I know exactly how you feel,' sympathized Larry. 'But at least you'll be back in the saddle soon, not like me. I had to wait a whole three months. Bit of a shock though, come and ride Mouse he'll put a smile back on your face.'

'Then Rollo,' offered Paul.

'And Jasper,' piped up Jack.

'I'll lead you over to Larry's on Donald. You're bound to be nervous at first but you know he's safe,' smiled Philip and kissed me lightly on the cheek, which made the others laugh and groan.

Not to be outdone Rose and Emma offered their ponies, but I said I would look silly with my long legs almost touching the floor.

'I've got a much better idea. Why not borrow Moon.' We all looked at Amy. 'At Easter we're all going on a cruise and I need to find someone to look after and ride her.'

Delighted, I threw off the blanket covering my legs and got off the sofa. 'Oh Amy, let's ask my mum and dad.'

***

'So you are absolutely sure that you still want a pony?'

They must have asked me that same question a hundred times, but I knew my parents were still worried following my accident, so I smiled and nodded.

'Of course. I know just the pony I would like. I've ridden him several times before and he is perfect for me. It went well having Moon here while Amy went on holiday, didn't it?'

'It did. So well in fact that Mrs Jennings is going to move Moon here, and pay us for a stable and grazing. Then you girls can both ride out after school.'

I gave them both a hug. 'That is wonderful news.'

'To put our minds to rest we've spoken to Squire Gray, and he has agreed to have the pony you choose up at the Hall for a week. Philip says he will give him or her a thorough trial. You don't mind?'

I gave my mother another hug. 'Of course not. Philip will love him like I already do.'

Two weeks later on a sunny May morning, Squire Gray's horsebox turned into the stable yard, the ramp was let down and my dream pony steadily walked off the ramp, dark conker coat gleaming with his bushy mane and tail plaited and woven with coloured ribbons. Those honest brown eyes smiled at me and I threw my arms around Gem's neck.

'Another Donald,' grinned Philip. 'I knew you would pick a good one and such good paces.'

Did Upper Valley Blue win the dressage, of course, the whole of the summer and the highly sought after Hill Trophy, after all Gem was the perfect pony.

ARACHNOPHOBIA

Rosemarie Czarnocka

Lizzie had been looking after the house and cat for her parents who were on holiday in Cornwall. They were not altogether happy about leaving the house unoccupied for two weeks, but she had persuaded them that they needed a change of scenery and the house and cat would be well cared for in their absence. She herself lived a short bus ride away so she could keep an eye on her own flat and carry on doing her part time job as a school dinner lady at the same time. She had agreed to sleep at her parents' house as they felt it would deter burglars and frankly Lizzie felt they were being rather paranoid, although she didn't want them to worry and spoil their first holiday in years. They were coming back in two days' time and she was vacuuming and dusting to make them feel welcome on their return home.

As she dusted she hummed a tune to herself half listening to a news bulletin on the radio. Suddenly she heard the word 'spider' and turned up the volume.

'This is a warning to people living in the London area of the escape from the zoo of a highly poisonous spider which is twice the size of a tarantula, the bite of which could prove fatal.

If found the spider should be approached with extreme caution, isolated and the zoo contacted immediately with a view to its capture and removal.'

Lizzie had a phobia about spiders and was horrified as it slowly dawned on her that this one in particular had escaped with the sole intention of coming after her and was desperate to find *it* before *it* found her. Armed with thick gardening gloves and a sharp pointed knife with which to kill it she began the search. She had no compunction whatsoever about killing a rare specimen. As far as she was concerned it was simply a matter of self-preservation.

"Where to start?" she asked herself out loud. She was in the habit of talking to herself when in a panic or faced with a worrying problem.

She decided to start downstairs and work her way to the top of the house. She started with the outhouse which was a lean-to housing the outside toilet in a very small brick building which was situated next to the outside door of the kitchen. This was a favourite haunt of insects, but, to her relief, there was no huge spider. The outhouse was always damp and sometimes in the morning big slugs would be found leaving their silvery trails behind them. Lizzie's mother usually disposed of these by sprinkling them with salt, and this involved clearing up the jelly residue and washing the cement floor.

The kitchen had an uneven concrete floor which provided several possible hiding places for the spider. She shone a torch behind the gas cooker, searched under the big butler sink and the large wooden dresser that held all the china and cooking utensils, and under the kitchen table and although she couldn't look behind the dresser she felt instinctively that the spider was not to be found in the kitchen.

The next room was the living room which was not very big and had three doors leading off it, one into the hall, one was a walk in larder and the other was the door to the cellar which ran under the front half of the entire house. She searched the room first but found nothing and she hesitated before tackling the cellar. All kinds of insects small and large found their way into this area of the house due mainly to the fact that at the far end was the coal chute the cover of which was in the front garden next to the bay window. The heavy metal cover had a fancy openwork pattern in it, but none of the holes were large enough to allow the entry of so huge a spider as she was seeking.

At the top of the wooden stairs her father's police uniform, helmet and truncheon were hung on coat hangers and hooks. She descended the stairs backwards so she could shine her torch into the dark space between the floor of the cupboard and the first step. Her hands were sweating and she had to grip the torch to prevent dropping it.

"What do I do if it leaps out at me?" she asked herself, but found no answer. Every inch of her flesh was crawling and her hands were shaking, but still no sign of the spider. She couldn't bear the thought of killing it when found, or of what this involved, but the alternative spurred her on.

Halfway down the stairs was a shelf with a curtain drawn across behind which were rows of preserving jars filled with fruit, jams, chutney, pickles and salted vegetables. She moved all the jars and let out a shriek as a large beetle scurried across the shelf looking for another hiding place. To the left of the shelf was a meat-safe which Lizzie's mother used instead of a fridge. It was always cool in the cellar. She didn't think the spider would be in the safe because it had fine mesh doors, but she was determined to leave no stone unturned.

Across the top of the cellar ceiling iron girders ran from wall to wall. Her father had a huge allotment which in 1939 had been two tennis courts end to end. Here he kept, pigs, chickens and rabbits and grew vegetables. At Easter and Christmas when he was allowed to keep two pigs for his own use, one for pork the other for bacon, the iron girders were hung with legs of pork and hams. The rest of his pigs were sold to the Ministry of Food during the war and later sent to market. The cellar had also served as two bedrooms during the war where the family slept and sheltered during the air raids and where Lizzie's youngest sister, Beth, had been born during a buzz bomb raid.

Lizzie pulled herself together and stopped reminiscing. She needed to concentrate on what she had to do and to be as prepared as possible. She resumed the search looking into every nook and cranny. She felt something fall on her head and screamed tearing wildly at her hair then realized it was a mass of tangled cobwebs she had walked into in the dim light. She had a few face to face encounters with several spiders of different sizes, but strangely enough these didn't seem to bother her as much as they would have before.

The search in the hall and front sitting room proved fruitless and by this time she was beginning to feel very exhausted. She felt sick with fear, her legs were trembling and she decided against anything to eat or drink but made her way upstairs looking carefully in the corners of each step. Immediately to the left at the top of the stairs was a large front bedroom which extended over the width of the house and where she and her sisters had all slept as small children and was also the room she was using while her parents were away from home. She decided she would leave this room to last.

Opposite the door to the large room was the door leading to one of the two smaller back bedrooms. This room had a built in cupboard and small fireplace apart from the usual bed, wardrobe and old fashioned wash stand with a marble top together with a wash basin and jug. It was used as the sick room when she or any of her sisters were ill and had to be isolated from the rest of the family. She didn't find what she was looking for in that room or the other one along the landing next to the bathroom.

"Where are you? Show yourself," she shouted. She was angry, terrified and completely worn out both mentally and physically.

Wearily Lizzie made her way back along the landing to the large front bedroom to continue the search. Fist she looked all-round the fireplace with the marble surround, then the built in cupboard on top and inside. Finally she shook the curtains and looked under the bed, wardrobe and dressing table with three hinged mirrors. She found nothing, but the day had been fraught with anxiety and panic and she was desperately tired. She began to wonder if she had been correct in thinking the spider in question was after her. London was such a big place and it could be anywhere. All she wanted to do was climb into bed and sleep. She undressed, drew back the bedclothes and sank into bed and within minutes she was in a deep, but troubled sleep.

    She woke next morning and her first thought was how silly she had been and what a lot of unnecessary work she had made for herself. She was feeling very drowsy and tried to stretch but couldn't move her legs, arms, head and body which seemed to be paralysed. She smiled to herself. What an idiot she was. It was obvious that she had been restless during the night and had the duvet twisted round her. With great effort she opened her eyes and discovered she was lashed to the bed by strong, sticky rope which she slowly realized with horror was the web of the huge spider, which she could see now sitting on the web in front of her head. She couldn't scream. Her vocal chords were also paralysed. All she could do was close her eyes and wait for the end.

A VERY SPECIAL CAT

Anne F. Clarke

A watery sun rose in the east beyond the line of oak trees which shielded the big straw barn and with it came the bitter cold of the east wind. A little half grown black cat huddled in the ditch wondering if she dare risk the open yard before she got to the warmth and safety of the barn.

She realised her mistake now. How could she have been so stupid? The big tabby tom with the torn ear she had seen yesterday, was right behind her in the ditch. He had smelt her scent from the spinney in the hundred acre field and tracked her to the side of the barn. She didn't stand a chance. He jumped on her, beat her into submission and after mating, left the little cat where he had found her, in the dirt of the ditch.

Trembling with fear and pain she walked across the yard and climbed as high as she could into the relative safety of the straw. The black cat fell into an exhausted sleep then woke in the afternoon thirsty, and with an empty belly.

***

Becky and Sara walked across the yard towards the barn. The cat watched them warily. Sara was carrying something.

'I'm sure I saw it Mum. It was black with two white paws. It looked really thin. Poor little thing.'

'Well,' said Sara, 'we don't want to frighten it. We'll just put the water and food inside the door and see if the little cat eats it.'

'Can't I give it some of the chicken we had for supper last night? I didn't eat all mine. I know there's some left in the fridge.' Becky looked up at her mother, her eyes appealing to the woman's generosity.

'We'll see,' said Sara. 'It might not be brave enough to come to the door. Let's go indoors and you can watch from the kitchen window.'

Inside the house the child climbed on to a kitchen chair and stared. Her eyes became tired with looking but, just before she turned away from the window, she saw a flash of black fur near the barn door.

'Mum,' she said in excitement, 'come quick. I've seen the little cat. It's eating the food we put down.'

Sara leant over the Becky's shoulder straining her eyes to look at the darkening yard. 'Where?'

'There, near the door frame.' said Becky 'Look, it's really hungry.'

Sara and Becky peered at the cat through the gloom of the January afternoon. They watched her eat greedily from the bowl and each hoped that the food would fill her empty belly and warm her thin body.

Just as they saw the cat finish the bowl of food and drink from the water bowl they heard the roar of a tractor engine and saw the glare of its headlights light up the yard. The light and noise startled her and she disappeared back into the darkness of the barn.

Early the next morning Becky collected the now empty bowls and placed fresh bowls of food and water on the loose straw of the barn floor. She quietly returned to the house and waited by the back door. She saw the cat watching her from the safety of the straw then hunger made the little creature bold and she crept closer to the bowl. The child slowly moved inside the door, looked through the little window at the top and saw the cat start to eat.

'Mum,' she called softly, 'Mum, she's still in the barn. I took the food over and she's eating it. Look, she's come down from the straw.'

'Yes,' said the woman, 'I can see her clearly this morning. She's quite a pretty little thing or she would be if she weren't so thin.'

'I thought,' said the child, looking sideways at the woman. 'I thought Mum, if I fed her every morning she might start to trust me. She wouldn't be thin anymore and we could keep her. Couldn't we?'

Sara smiled at her. 'I expect so Becky, but she is wild so you mustn't be disappointed if she doesn't want to stay. Mind you, she would keep the mice out of the stables and she's got big ears. They're always the sign of a good mouser!' The child sensed her victory and so continued to feed the cat.

Each morning Becky placed the food in the barn and waited a few feet away. After the cat had eaten she let the child move a little closer. Weeks passed and the trust between the cat and the child grew. Becky was now able to kneel down, stretch out her arm and tentatively touch the black fur with her finger. However, any sudden noise made the cat retreat into the darkness of the barn.

On a rainy Sunday morning, Becky carried a bowl of food to the barn and waited as usual. No cat. She listened and heard a mewling sound coming from the cat's straw nest. She walked towards the noise, climbed up the bales and there tucked up inside the straw she saw the cat. It was not alone. There were two kittens, tiny and blind, suckling the mother cat.

Becky backed slowly and quietly out of the barn then ran as fast as she could back to the house. She kicked off her boots, flung open the door and ran to the foot of the stairs.

'Mum, Mum come quick. The cat, it's got kittens. They're so tiny. Quick, come and see.'

'Ok, ok, Becky. I'm coming.'

Sara ran down the stairs and followed her daughter through the kitchen to the back door. They walked across the yard together.

'Let's be really quiet,' said Sara. 'We mustn't frighten her. She might leave the kittens if we interfere.'

'I know that.' whispered Becky, 'Look, Mum, look. Aren't they sweet? I can't believe how tiny they are.'

The woman and child smiled at each other and quietly watched the little wild family.

'Come on, Becky,' said Sara. 'Let's leave them alone then the cat can feed. She'll be too scared if we're here. You can come back at tea time.'

Becky fed the cat every day as usual and watched the kittens grow. The smallest one was black like its mother and the biggest, tabby with white paws. Their mother was still wary of humans but tolerated the child's touch and continued to feed and drink from the bowls. Soon the kittens could see. They stared at the child with curiosity, wide eyed and trusting.

As the spring days grew warmer the mother cat risked hunting at night. One night when the kittens were four weeks old and almost weaned, she left them safe in their straw bale nest near the door frame. The cat crossed the yard and moved quietly along the side of the stackyard to the stables. She could smell mice in the feed shed. She had killed three mice when she caught the scent of the tom cat.

Fear made her fast. She raced back past the stackyard to the yard. Her kittens were alone and defenceless. The big tabby cat might kill them if he found them. She forgot about the tractor in the yard. The driver didn't see her in the dark. His front wheel hit her and knocked her sideways into the wall of the barn. Despite her desperate injuries she managed to crawl towards the straw and her kittens. They moved closer to her sniffing her bloodied black fur mewling and pushing at her teats. They circled her unresponsive body.

Dawn broke behind the line of oak trees, sunlight streamed through the cracks in the barn wall turning the straw gold. The kittens left the cold body of their mother and crept out into the yard towards the backdoor of the farmhouse. It took them a long time to reach the door step, hunger and thirst slowed their progress. Instinct pushed them towards the child.

Becky woke early that Sunday morning. She dreamed that someone was crying and woke up suddenly. Someone was crying. It sounded like a cat. She threw off the bed clothes, put a sweatshirt over her pyjamas and ran down the stairs, through the kitchen to the back door. Something made her hesitate as she went to open it. She looked down through the small window in the top half of the door and saw the kittens huddled together on the step.

Becky opened the backdoor carefully then bent down and picked up the tiny bundles of fluff and bone and carried them into the kitchen. She put a kitchen towel in a box she found in the pantry and set the box and kittens on the floor next to the Aga. She ran upstairs into her mother's room and shook her awake.

'Wake up Mum, wake up. I've found the kittens on the door step. They're really hungry but I can't see the mother anywhere. Please come down and help me.'

Sara got out of bed, put on her dressing gown and followed the child downstairs to the kitchen. She smiled when she saw the kittens. She found all young things enchanting.

'Right Becky,' she said, 'We need to get some liquid into these kittens, they are dehydrated. There's some powdered milk in the pantry on the middle shelf. We'll mix it with some boiled water and feed them with that little pipette I use for the baby pigs.'

Becky took the kettle off the Aga and poured a little of the water in a cup, found the powdered milk and mixed both with a small whisk to a thin liquid so that it wouldn't choke the kittens. Sara drew the liquid up into the pipette and put a drop onto the back of her hand.

'It's not too hot,' she said. 'Give me the little black one first.' She held him and dripped the liquid into the side of his mouth. He mewed and spat but managed to swallow a little. The tabby kitten seemed stronger and swallowed more.

Becky put the kittens back into the box near the warmth of the Aga. She looked at her mother.

'If I feed them every hour do you think they'll be alright Mum? And if they are alright in the morning can I ask the Vet to look at them when he comes tomorrow? I mean, just so he can check they're alright.' She looked intently at Sara.

'We'll see in the morning, Becky. Don't get your hopes too high. This little black one seems very weak. Now I must dress and get breakfast and you must go outside and look in the barn for the mother cat. I can't think why she's left them.'

Becky put on her boots, crossed the yard and went into the barn. She found the still black body in the straw nest the cat had made for her kittens. The black fur was streaked with blood where the tractor wheel had hit her. She gently picked up the little cat and carried her to the kitchen garden and looked around for a special place to bury her.

Sara was hanging sheets on the linen line. She stopped and stroked the cold, black, furry body that the child held in her arms.

'I think the tractor wheel hit her last night Mum.' she said, trying hard not to cry. 'I saw the tyre marks near the barn wall. Where shall I put her?'

'Somewhere sunny. What about near the fruit cage. Would you like me to help you?' The woman stroked the child's hair.

'No, it's alright. I can do it. She tried so hard to live, didn't she Mum?'

The earth was soft and loose near the raspberry canes. Becky managed very well with a trowel she found discarded by the greenhouse and buried the mother cat in a shallow grave. She wiped away her tears with a muddy hand and sat down on the grass near the linen line.

'You know Mum, I'm used to our animals being born and living and dying but this feels different. I did love that little cat.' She whispered. 'I really did.'

The kittens survived the night.

In the morning the woman said, 'Becky, Frank the vet will be here soon to do some pregnancy tests on the pigs. You can go outside and tell him to come in for a coffee when he's finished and then he can look at the kittens.'

The child fed the kittens with the pipette, put them back in their box and went out into the yard. She found the vet and their farm manager in the big farrowing house. She hung about for a few minutes and then between tests asked the Vet to come into the house before he went home. He smiled at her and wondered why she looked so anxious.

'Come in and sit down, Frank,' said Sara. 'Here's your coffee. How were the tests?'

'Pretty satisfactory,' said Frank, 'but I think you should replace two of your boars. When I come next month I'll need to check your mortality rates too.' He drank his coffee. 'Well Becky,' he said, 'what have you got to show me?'

Becky picked up the box and put the kittens on the table.

'Could you have a look at my kittens, please,' she said. 'Mum thinks the black one might die. What do you think?'

'Tell you what, Becky,' said Frank the vet. 'I'll take them back to the surgery now and I'll do some tests and get some liquid into them. Then I'll get my nurse to give you a ring tomorrow.'

'I've been thinking about what to call them.' said Becky. 'Are they boys or girls?' The vet took another look. 'Both boys, I think.'

'I thought, because they've been so brave, I mean they got across the yard and found us, all by themselves, that they should be called after someone famous,' Becky hesitated. 'So, I've decided on Montgomery and Nelson. Nelson's the tabby. Do you think that's ok?'

'Big names for such tiny creatures,' said the Vet smiling, 'take them out to my car Becky. You'll get a call tomorrow.'

Becky thought about the kittens all day. The vet nurse from the surgery rang the next morning. Sara spoke to her whilst Becky stood by listening intently.

'What did she say, Mum. Are they alright?'

'Well, yes and no.' said Sara. 'The little black one you called Montgomery died in the night. He was too dehydrated and too weak to save. But,' she hesitated looking at Becky's stricken face. 'Nelson is fine and we can pick him up at the end of the week.'

'Oh, Mum,' she said, flinging herself into her mother's arms. 'I knew something good would happen. Can we bring Monty home and bury him with his mother?' Sara nodded, blew her nose on an old tissue she found in her pocket and hugged the child back.

They buried the black kitten, near the raspberry canes next to his mother.

***

'When can we bring Nelson home, Mum?' said the child a few days later.

'Becky, you've asked me that every morning this week. I'll ring the surgery on Friday morning. Then we can bring him home after we done the shopping.' said Sara. 'I suppose he'll need a cage to travel in.'

'And one of those round squashy beds to sleep in.' said Becky hoping the shopping money could be stretched to include suitable possessions for her new treasure.

Sara laughed. 'Who's paying? Me or you?'

'I've still got some of my birthday money left and last week's pocket money. I could get him one of those squeaky toys as well.' Her daughter's excitement touched Sara after the sadness of the last week.

They brought Nelson home on Friday afternoon.

'Look at him Mum, he's really grown and he's not a bit afraid.' said Becky as she watched the kitten exploring every corner of the kitchen. 'I think,' she said seriously, 'he's going to be a very special cat.'

'Well,' said Sara, 'He must have used up at least four of his nine lives already.' She picked the kitten up and stroked his stripy head and ears. 'He's going to have a nice quiet life from now on.'

The kitten grew into a handsome cat. His life with on the farm was comfortable and mostly quiet. He and Becky were inseparable. She loved him, spoiled him and worried about him.

'It's no good Becky,' said Sara in exasperation one evening, 'you cannot keep Nelson in at night. He wants to go out hunting. It's natural for him. And I wish you wouldn't let him sleep on your bed. And don't look at me like that I know you do, I've seen the muddy paw marks.'

Becky looked defiantly at Sara. 'If he's on my bed Mum I know he's safe. Anyway he doesn't need to go out. I mean he's not hungry or anything and I only let him upstairs when he cries.'

'Well,' said Sara, 'I'll leave the kitchen window ajar tonight and he can go out if he wants to and on Friday we'll buy a cat flap. Now off to bed with you!'

The child glared at her mother in annoyance and ran up the stairs. Once in bed she kept herself awake by playing games on her ipod. She quickly pushed it under the pillow and feigned sleep when Sara came in to say goodnight. Becky waited until the house was quiet before she crept down the stairs and across the hall to the kitchen. Opening the door she saw Nelson on the window sill. Her voice became soft and persuasive.

'Come on Nelson, look what I've got.' and she rustled the bag of treats she kept on the dresser for him. The cat's yellow eyes fixed on the food as she walked towards him. Her hand reached out slowly as if to caress him, he leaned towards her and wham! Becky clutched him tightly in her arms.

'Gotcha!' she cried and carried him upstairs to her room. Nelson made himself comfortable on the duvet, kneaded it with his paws and slept. The child smiled to herself, put her arm around the cat and slept too.

Becky dreamed of journeys and adventures and then of a wood but the trees were burning. She was coughing, she couldn't run away and all the time she could hear Nelson crying. She could feel his head pushing at her face.

Then she woke to find her bedroom half full of thick acrid smoke. Becky grabbed Nelson and crawled to the door. She reached up and opened it. The smoke was billowing up the stairs and onto the landing. She stood up.

'Mum, Mum,' she screamed. Her mother's bedroom door was ajar, smoke curling round the door frame. Nelson leapt out of the child's arms, shot through the doorway and landed on the Sara's bed. She woke up to find Becky and Nelson pulling her out of bed. She smelled the smoke and felt the heat downstairs.

'Becky, I think the kitchen's on fire. I can hear it crackling! Shut the door quick. I'm going to open the window and throw the duvet and pillows onto the flower bed. Then we'll throw the mattress out and we'll jump. Nelson, you can go first.'

Sara flung the duvet and pillows out of the window, grabbed the cat, leaned down as far as she could and let him go. He landed easily amidst the delphiniums. Sara and Becky heaved the mattress off the bed and started to push it through the window.

'Mum it's caught on a nail. It won't move.'

'It's ok, Becky. Just push as hard as you can.' Her mother's voice was reassuring and strong. 'Look, it's moving.' They both heard a ripping, tearing sound as the mattress finally sailed out of the window.

'Right Becky aim for the mattress. When you're down, you and Nelson run to the office pick up the phone and dial 999. Now jump!'

The child hit the mattress with a thud. Then cat and child ran across the garden to the farm office. Becky shut Nelson in the office kitchen. She went back into the main office, picked up the telephone and dialled 999 for the emergency services.

'Which service do you require?' announced the operator.

'I think we need the fire brigade,' Becky said 'our kitchen is on fire and my Mum has just jumped out of her bedroom window. She'll be here in a minute.'

'Tell me your name, address and telephone number, dear.' said the operator just as Sara appeared in the doorway.

'Mum, I've told the lady we need a fire engine. I think she wants to talk to you.' said Becky handing the telephone to Sara.

'Hello,' she said. 'Yes, it's Sara Jenkins, Holly Tree Farm, IP21 6QT. We're just off the B1132.' Sara winced as she sat down in front of the office desk.

'Are you hurt?' said the operator. 'Do you need an ambulance as well?'

'I'm not sure. When I jumped out of my bedroom window I missed a bit of the mattress and landed on my shoulder. I think I may have broken my collar bone.' She grinned in spite of her pain.

'We're all fine, really. Although I'm not sure about the kitchen! Do you need the grid reference?'

'No,' said the operator, 'I've found you on the computer. The fire service are on their way and I'll call the paramedics just in case. Take care.'

'Put the kettle on Becky.' said Sara. 'I think we both need a cup of tea.'

Becky opened the door to the office kitchen and found Nelson looking worried so she gave him a saucer of milk on the office desk then went back into the kitchen and put the kettle on. By the time the fire engine arrived she had made tea for Sara and herself.

***

'Well,' said the fire officer with the white helmet. 'The fire's out but your kitchen is a mess. We think it started with your dishwasher. Did you leave it on last night Mrs Jenkins?'

Sara thought hard. 'Yes, I think I turned it on before I went to bed.'

The fireman looked at her. 'What I can't understand is why your smoke alarms didn't go off.'

'I can.' she said. 'The one on the landing needs a new battery. I got a new one on Friday but forgot to put it in and there isn't one in the kitchen.'

'I would strongly advise you to fit some new smoke alarms. You were lucky to get out of your house alive.' said the fire officer frowning at her. 'Who woke you up?'

Sara and Becky looked at Nelson sitting on the office desk drinking his milk. 'He did!' they said in unison. 'He's our very special cat.'

COMPLIMENTS OF THE SHOOTING SEASON

John Antram

Hunting-gathering man.
In fruit and nut filled days,
Finds a fine October pleasant
For his winter storage eating
While solar heating comforts are depleting.

Less fortunate is the pheasant
Whose darkest hours begin. Non-native
Brought here from sub-continental Raj
To breed, and thrive, and fly, to satisfy
The rich man's blood lust,
Tamed by 'keeper's' daily feeding.

The month commences; custom
Now compounds the sin:
Guns come out and brothers, sisters,
All begin, alarmed, in pain and terrified,
To die. I cry: Walk, Don't fly!

May game-bird spirit realms
In partnership with angels, and their chums,
Bring this barbaric mayhem to an end
With cool pedestrianisation scheme
Evolved to spike the guns
Get shot of this charade. While hunger
Doesn't drive these so-called sportsmen
Shooting for the pot they are not.

The year goes round. As February starts
Another irony is witnessed:
Game birds breathe more easily
As shootings of the shallow men must end
When greening shoots of spring begin again

FENLAND INCIDENT

Judith Osborne

His brain snapped to attention. Was that a rough snore from his right?

Left foot slurping from the mud to meet the right one, Fraser stopped in the waist-high tufted, marshy grass he had been picking a track through. His brain registered in front of him stunted trees, twisted branches, a few taller, leaning, stretching. Could anyone sleep on this sodden ground? Who would want to? Third snore; but no shape of a person visible.

He swallowed. He really didn't want to draw attention to himself by clearing his throat just yet. Not until he was more confident, then he could turn from any waking monster, run, and start shouting to his parents back in camp.

His nose tickled. A great big sneeze was climbing round the back, making his eyelids clench, and he grabbed to pinch his nostrils hard. But you can't make a completely silent sneeze. You can't, and in the same second as his best effort - a choking snort - violent rustling and waving of the grass made him try to extract a sodden foot from the treacly sludge to back away.

Mistake! He stumbled clumsily, tried to grab a root, bent his right wrist back as he half fell.

Pain, filthy muddy hands, dirty splashed sleeves, sodden shoes. He straightened a bit, holding the throbbing wrist, shot a quick look to work out who or what was lurking, lumbering away. A thing. A brown, bristly thing. Couldn't be a porcupine, wrong country. Couldn't be a beaver.

Oh Lord - a giant RAT? OK fine, do they snore? No idea, but can they run! They have huge sharp teeth as well. They slither, and there are always THOUSANDS OF THEM after you've seen just one.

Almost sobbing with wrist pain, tripping over ankle-wrenching knobbly roots and tufty wet grass, Fraser was grunting with effort. Mud-soaked cold heavy shoes. Was it getting more difficult to peer through the trees ahead? What was that noise in the sky? He couldn't see properly. Oh, a chopper circling. He had the mad thought, was it looking for an escaped prisoner, with him out here alone? Oh, no!

Every step was a lurch, a squelch, a stumble. Which way now? His left hand clawing and trying to push a way into the little bunch of bushes and small trees, he was being beaten by jumbled, flailing branches. Sudden rattling pushy gusts of chilling wind, and not a landmark to recognise.

Was that a sob?

Oh, his own sob. He must stand still and THINK.

Featureless, blank swampy ground surrounded the straggly trees, but there _are_ landmarks: there are _always_ landmarks. THINK. He had to try to remember particular clumps of trees, shapes of bushes.

Was that chopper moving away or getting nearer?

Was there one really tall tree? He had to look properly: turn all the way round. The drizzle wasn't really enough to stop anyone seeing clearly. In fact there was a tiny bit of blue sky over there. Was that where the brightest bit was? If so that's where the sun was and it must be in the south. Now clouds were tanking across again. Gusts of wind, rattle and swish of branches and leaves filled his ears.

Muffled roar of that chopper. Surely it was circling nearer and nearer.

It couldn't be looking for HIM could it? How long had he been gone? Then he thought, No, stupid, not been away anything like long enough. Oh! Change of engine noise; blades clanking instead of whirring. Oh, no! Something's wrong; it's coming down, and very near.

Hands clenched tightly, head lowered, his eyes darted around to try to see exactly where the thing was going to finally land. Nowhere to hide, nowhere to run in the swamp.

In a deafening, ear-splitting moment of thuds and crashes, a tornado of wind from the blades, and a peculiar smell of something like petrol, it was down, to his right. Blades suddenly still. Startling silence of the engine.

Petrol smell? Who's in there? Anyone coming out? Come on, come out! He shouted inside his head, but nobody appeared. Blades still, engine off, better go and see what's happening.

A painful squelching muscle-aching trudge towards the stranded machine, his brain a bit frozen. What will there be to find? _Who_ will there be to find? He wondered. His breathing was laboured, legs ached. He was muddy, wet, half collapsing every few steps on to one knee or the other, trainer nearly off right foot, nose running, eyes lashed by strands of hair.

Keep going, he said to himself. The hatch is opening a bit, is it? Yes, I can hear a faint voice from inside calling, 'Anyone there? Anyone there? Oh, please!' and there's a hand waving a piece of cloth.

'Yes, here, coming!' They probably can't hear me, but hope, repeat it, against the tearing wind. Hatch slammed shut again. Hurl yourself against the side, bang good fist on the hatch. I can see two shapes through the window, one a girl, quite young, leaning over an adult in the next seat.

Rain sluicing and cascading down now. Keep up the banging on the chopper side. The hatch is opening a crack. Grab it, grip it. Ow, not with that hand! Force it further open. The young girl must be pushing from the inside.

'You OK? What's happened? What went wrong?' Make the words as loud and efficient as possible. Make them sound as if you could do something, not as if you're at the end of your tether, wrist throbbing madly after that banging, ankle not far off the same.

'My uncle's ill. He's been sick,' the girl says.

'I'll be fine in five minutes,' mutters a not very strong voice.

The girl throws an agitated and anxious look at her uncle.

'I think I made the radio work to get emergency services,' she says, 'but it went dead before I could hear an answer, and I can't get it back.'

'And I don't have my mobile. Stupid. What can I do? Better wait here to see if someone appears first.'

'Can you squeeze in here so you're out of the rain?'

I don't need a second invitation and scramble in. Very small space with two people already in. And the smell of sick's suffocating. The uncle looks rough. Yes, ill, in fact. 'Hi,' is all he manages.

'Hi. I'm Fraser.' Trying not to move my legs or arms in case of disturbing him.

The girl speaks in an unsteady voice, 'I'm Rachel. I'm really worried about Uncle Frank. He suddenly said he felt rotten and was violently sick. Don't know how he got us down. I've only been able to wipe his face. I've got nothing more to clean up with. You're really wet and filthy. How did you get here?'

'Don't worry. Er, if we open the hatch just a bit we'll hear if someone's coming for us. Is there anything to jam it open with? If not, I'll stand with my back to it and keep it a tiny bit open, but not so we all get soaked.'

'I think that's what you'll have to do; it's not easy to prop open.'

'OK, done.' At least a thread of air comes in to freshen things. And it's also true we do stand a better chance of hearing any rescuers. Now I'm wondering what that extra rumbling roar is mixed in with the wind and rain? Another chopper? Could it be?

Rachel looks pretty awful herself now. 'I'm going to get out for a minute' I say. The hatch door slams behind me. I look up; strain ears and eyes, and yes, a bigger chopper emerging from the navy blue-black cloud. Could be yellow. Yellow chopper equals Air Ambulance. Oh, wow! I bang on the door again, jab a finger up at the sky and mouth words about the chopper through the window.

Big, cumbersome, head-splittingly noisy, the helicopter sits in the air almost above us. The down draught from the propellers tears at clothing, hair, grass, bushes; from the opened door a bulky person starts to descend through the wet air and wind on a snaking, twisting cable, that dumps him on the rough ground.

I hear the yell, 'O.K. mate?' See a hand raised in salute, and decide I'm allowed to feel relieved for a minute, before I worry about the trouble I'll undoubtedly be in from my parents.

GIVE A DOG A BONUS

John Antram

The Labrador pup had run, so full of fun.
From sunlit garden just when sunbeams on the house
Betrayed a window, where a bright venetian blind
Is hung behind.
But Brad is out of luck; his head is stuck.
The slats have slotted round his throat and
He has torn his ear.

The handyman arrived after the vet, who has applied
An airline to protruding canine face.
The tube, the switch, the slanting shafts of white
Are not so clear as sweet intake of light, life-giving air
In all this lack of dignity: one saving grace.

A THIEF?

Judith Osborne

Polly's room was sharply cold.

She flung herself through the door, sobbing. There was nothing there to make her feel better. Nothing to welcome her. The curtains were still half pulled. Her bed was messy with a mix of shoes, clothes, soft toys. DVDs, CDs and magazines had slid across the small table she used as a desk.

She slumped heavily across her bed. One hand grasped at her sheet to find a bit of warmth and comfort. She needed it. She'd been found out in something really wrong.

Other girls taking on dares had always seemed stupid to her. Why, oh why, had she taken on this one?

Tom was watching and listening, that was why. She so needed his admiring gaze. It made her feel good, even clever, and that didn't happen too often.

It was a joke at the time. Tom had been smiling.

Nobody liked Mrs Marvellous Moira Murray. History teacher. Who in their right mind wanted to hear what went on 300 years ago? Nobody. Plus Murray was a Scot. You didn't always catch what she was saying first time. She had told Polly off last week. She'd dropped her bag of books at the top of the stairs and Murray said she was 'playing the wee fool'. Really that mad Eric had pushed her. But Murray hadn't listened to Polly, same as she didn't listen to her in class.

Waste of space, wasn't she? Needed to be shown she wasn't as clever as Polly's class.

Linda was the one who'd spotted Murray's handbag. She had shouted to her four friends, Tom, Polly, Bethany and Bob,

'Yuck! Bet she loves that thing. Old and ugly, her and her bag – two old bags together, eh? Why not give her a shock? Make it disappear? Dare you, Polly! Go on, dare you! I've seen her leave it on the side table in the dining room. She goes into the office next door. Easy peasy. If anyone sees you, they'll back you up when they know whose bag you're taking.'

Tom had smiled that warm smile. It made Polly feel life was better. She had a friend.

'Right,' she'd said, 'OK. I'll do it. Serve her right. Will you help me watch for when she leaves the bag?' Linda and Bethany had agreed.

She'd only had to wait two days. Bethany had run up behind her on the way from Maths to English. She said Mrs Murray was just round the corner. It looked like she was going to put her bag on that side table.

Polly had felt a bit sick then. At the same time she was fired up. She nipped round the corner. Mrs Murray was taking papers out of her dark blue bag. She left the bag on the table. She even turned away from where Polly had stood still for a second. Murray hadn't seen her. She closed the office door behind her with a sharp click.

A swift look both ways. Coast clear. Polly took three steps up to the table. She gripped the dark blue bag. Turned away very fast. Pushed the thing up her body warmer. Zipped up very fast. About ten seconds of clever work, that was. There had been a bit of danger. Only a very little bit of danger.

And now it was Monday and she knew that a pair of eleven year old eyes had been watching her. An eleven year old tongue had been wagging. Everyone knew.

She felt like a little girl inside her head, wanting her mummy to say,

'Hush, darling, there's nothing to worry about. Mummy's here. The hurt will go away very soon.'

She sobbed loudly again: it wasn't that simple. She was now a teenager with a real problem. She had been found out in something really wrong. Plus she didn't have a mummy who kissed her better.

Horrible Helen, the woman her father had married last year, didn't want her there. She only wanted her father to be there.

Sometimes Polly said she was bored and didn't know what to do next. Every time that happened Helen chanted at her in a singsong voice,

'Polly put the kettle on!' as if that was a real answer.

She'd finally been driven to ask Dad why Helen did it. He'd smiled and said it was 'funny and nice' to have a verse with her name in it. He said she was being silly to be so upset. As usual Dad was not understanding her. He was on the side of Helen.

How could Polly not be upset and angry? It was a nursery rhyme. That meant Helen thought of her as a nursery kid, didn't it? Even the kids at school hadn't chanted stupid verses like that at her.

What chance did she have of getting through any of her problems now?

Was that the best Helen had to offer her?

Polly had always liked her own name before. She remembered her mum calling her on summer days in the garden,

'Polly, dear, time to come in now.'

That always meant she got a little cake that her mum had baked. She'd run in quickly with a smile on her face.

Nothing left to smile about now.

No Mummy to run to now.

She shivered with cold and fear. Sobbed again.

She grabbed tissues from under her pillow. She blew her nose hard, tears still blinding her.

Now she felt a bit sick. Had she eaten anything? No idea. What did it matter anyway?

Did she want to listen to her music? No.

Well, just maybe. Loud, to drown out her worry. But Horrible Helen would come up to shout at her.

It had to be headphones. Don't know where they are. Too cold to look.

Must she think about her big problem? Was it worth making your brain hurt for?

She'd been found out. By an eleven year old.

A tap on the door, a voice, and the door opening.

Oh, no! Oh, no! What could be worse than Horrible Helen coming barging in? What now?

'Polly, are you OK? You ran upstairs without saying 'Hi!' or anything. Are you crying? What's the problem? Tell me if you can – I really want to help.'

'You can't help!' Polly shouted, banging her fists into the pillow. 'You can't help!' she repeated. 'You don't know how to and you don't know me. You'd hate me even more if I told you…'

'Oh, Polly, come on, dear, give me a chance. I absolutely don't hate you and if I can hear the story, at least I promise I'll think about what's possible. We can think together.'

Polly hardly took in the words, her own sobs were so loud. Her horror so huge at the idea that she might have to tell Helen. And she was so freezing cold.

'Put a sweater on and come downstairs where it's a bit warmer. I'll make hot chocolate. Come on – here's a sweater, over your head, give me your hand.'

Helen half pulled Polly, stumbling down the stairs into the kitchen and a bit of warmth.

'Is your problem at school? Has someone been nasty to you?' Helen said, as she put on the milk and dropped chocolate powder into Polly's favourite red and white mug.

'No, no! I can't tell you. I can't tell you. You'll hate me –'

'Now, Polly, darling, stop that. I don't hate you and I never will. There is nothing at all about you to hate; you're a really nice girl, and I want us to enjoy ourselves together.'

'Well you won't be able to love me. I'm a thief!' Polly's shriek of anguish hit the walls of the kitchen and bounced back. 'Thief! Thief! Thief! Thief!

A black pit of silence.

Polly's eyes were glued to Helen's, while she shook in every limb and started to shred a tissue.

The End. The End. It must be the End. There was no going back.

She would have to run away. And she hadn't even spoken to her father first.

Helen looked stiff and uncomfortable. Not loving, but quiet. She wasn't shouting; she wasn't running out of the house, slamming the door behind her – yet. But she hadn't heard the story yet, either. Helen's voice was a bit husky and there was a space between each word as she said,

'Oh, Polly, I don't think I believe that.'

'I am! I am! But it was going to be a joke, but it wasn't and I don't know what to do.'

'You need to tell me the whole story. Here's your chocolate – just sip it, it's hot. Sit down and take a couple of deep breaths before you start talking.'

Polly tried. She kept shuddering, but she managed all the bits of the story that had led up to the dare. Just Tom's name did not come in to it. Mrs Marvellous Moira Murray, Linda, Bethany and Bob, yes. Just not Tom.

'The others were smiling and giggling, they knew I meant it to be a joke, really they did, and they said it was funny. 'Two old bags together', you know? They said everyone would understand anyway, because Mrs Murray's so horrible.'

'OK, Polly, and who do you say saw you? Someone from Year 7? Yes, OK, and of course she didn't know it was a dare, so when she saw the teacher's bag being taken she assumed it was a real theft – yes?'

'Yes, and she's told everybody, and now nobody will speak to me.'

This mental picture brought more sobs and made more tears flow down Polly's face. Helen leaned forward, and took both her hands;

'Polly, there are a few difficulties we have to deal with, not just whether any one in school is speaking to you, however awful that is. Firstly, where is the handbag, and its contents? Secondly, has Mrs Murray asked to see you?

'I brought the bag home overnight in my school bag after I'd shown it to Linda and everyone, then this morning I put it straight back on the table I got it from.'

'Did you see what was in the bag?'

'No'

'Are you sure?'

'Yes, I'm sure. I didn't want to know about it. It was too embarrassing'

'And Mrs Murray - ?'

Polly broke in, 'She's asked to see me tomorrow morning first thing. She may phone Dad as well. I'm so scared.'

'Dad will have to know, of course, but listen, we can do that together. We can help him understand how it happened – that does make a difference. But you tell me what you think is the very most important aspect to learn for yourself from it.'

'I should never have taken the dare.'

'Well and it's not just any old dare, it included taking someone's property. Completely not on. You've always been
told ...'

'I know, I know.'

'Well I'm glad it seems so obvious now. Perhaps remembering earlier might have helped. Can we start thinking what to do next?'

The silence that fell then was nothing like the deep, black pothole that had followed her shriek of 'Thief!' earlier. Could she stop weeping? If she was being asked to consider what to do next, maybe it was not 'the End'. It seemed there could still be a place for her in her own home. Life could continue. But it still felt empty and lonely inside her head and she didn't want to look Helen in the face.

She was upstairs again when her Dad came home at half past six as usual. Called 'Hi, Pol!' up the stairs to her in her room. Also as usual.

Her silly, croaky voice and tense stomach muscles were not as usual.

She expected him to come upstairs to find out what was wrong, but Helen must have spoken quietly to get him to talk to her first. Polly stared numbly out of the window. Dare she go down straight away?

Yes, she dare. Dad was Dad. He might even give her a hug. She really needed a hug.

The staircase seemed somehow longer and difficult to deal with, her legs were so wobbly.

'I think you need to go up and hear it from her, Mark', she heard Helen saying in the kitchen, as she turned from the bottom stair to go in. And, no, he was not holding out his arms to her. He looked as if he didn't recognise her.

'Dad, oh Dad!' Polly gasped.

Her father said slowly, 'I need you to tell me the whole story'

'Helen's already told you...'

Her father broke in, 'Come on, Polly, just tell the story.'

And somehow she did, with gulps, in the feeble, croaky voice that she couldn't seem to clear. Once again, by the way, she didn't mention Tom. He needed to be kept a bit longer in a secret place in her brain.

'And I do know exactly how stupid I was,' she eventually finished a bit weakly, 'but I don't know what to do next.'

'First promise yourself, then promise me and Helen, never to consider doing such a thing again. Second, come and have a hug. Third we need to get supper.'

Ah! A Dad hug. What a relief. Then another – Helen held her very quietly, and sort of carefully.

'Help me get some supper?' she whispered.

As they ate, rather slowly and painfully, Dad came up with another bonus – he would be with her to see the Head, and Mrs Murray.

'But you explain yourself and apologise for yourself and then leave me to ask what we do next, OK? No TV tonight, of course. Early to bed, you need it. Read a bit, and set your alarm early enough to do any school work in the morning. And remember we're aiming that something good will come out of this mess you created. Focus! Right?'

'Focus!' – one of his favourite words. He and Helen were looking at her more normally. Was there a chance that 'normal' could return in a big way – well, at least at home? Linda, Bethany and Bob – any 'normal' from them possible? And Tom? Didn't bear thinking about, trying to tackle all that, and she wasn't going to try.

Her puffy eyelids finally closed. Sleep.

Porridge with golden syrup followed the hideous alarm clock and the fuzzy-brained hour of French and History homework – better keep Murray sweet on that score and not turn up to class without it.

The interview with the Head and Mrs Murray made her palms sweaty and her voice croaky and weak again. Both teachers stared at her as only teachers can, sending out waves of expecting something very different and very much saner than they were actually hearing.

Yes, it was about as bad an experience as she had foreseen.

Dad sitting staring at his feet, saying not a word, while she stood and struggled. But somehow her second, or was it third, apology for being so stupid and doing something so wrong, had been croaked out. Without letting on that she couldn't stand the History teacher standing in front of her. And without referring to Tom.

The Head let a silence fall (well, she would, wouldn't she? Wringing the last drop of effect out of the awful situation.) Then asked Mrs Murray if she would like to talk to Polly.

'I am horribly shocked and surprised, and I really would like to talk to you on your own at morning break. Please come and ask for me at the staff room.'

'Yes, Mrs Murray.'

'On second thoughts. I shall be driving along your road after school to take my dog for a run on Bishop's Meadow. May I call in, Mr Graham, if

Polly and her Mum will be there?'

Dog? Mrs Murray had a dog? That was the best thing she'd heard about her by a long way. Dad said he would let Helen know that Mrs Murray was coming.

The Head repeated 'surprised and shocked' in her dismissal of Polly, but at least finished with,

'Now we must all do our best to move on. I will support you, Polly, and so will Mrs Murray. She will tell your class about the dare, I believe?'

'Yes, I shall say how wrong Linda, Bethany and Bob were to dare you, and ask them to make sure they support you now. My bag was back with me immediately, with all its contents, and I don't intend to prolong the agony.'

Polly's thanks were as burbled as her confession had been, and then she was out of the office. Straight into the corridor, now full of hurrying bodies heading for classrooms. She needed to get to Tom before Old Murray started her public Presentation, naming the darers, so she could assure Tom she hadn't included his name.

Keeping her head down and wondering exactly where and how she was going to manage to speak to Tom on her own, Polly made reasonable progress towards the banks of lockers near the library.

A chance he would be there. Was he? Yes – great!

'Tom, I must speak to you very quickly.' He looked uncomfortable and opened his mouth to speak.

'Tom, I've just seen the Head and Marvellous Murray about you-know-what. They know Linda, Bethany and Bob dared me, the Year 7 girl heard them talking about it. They don't know you were there at all. Murray's going to talk to the whole class. You don't need to say a thing.' In one rapid slide, she was on her way to the classroom, not looking back.

Then yet another shock to shake Polly rigid. As Marvellous Murray launched on her public Presentation about the Dare, Tom's voice –

'Mrs Murray, you need to add my name. I'm really sorry.'

Every beady little eye was fixed on him, a few feet shuffled: someone got a fit of coughing. What did he have to tell Murray that for? She, Polly, would have protected him, and he knew it. Stupid! Unbelievable!

Mrs Murray's voice was continuing firmly, having thanked Tom for his honesty. And two minutes later she'd finished. Done.

Lessons, break, lunch and few people in her class sought Polly out. Linda, Bethany and Bob were acceptably almost normal with her, but didn't actually apologise for their part in the fiasco. Tom smiled a bit tightly at her from a distance at lunch time, and otherwise made no effort to speak.

That school day was very long. Polly didn't want another any time soon. And she still had this peculiar visit at home from Mrs Murray and her dog to deal with.

Bombshell!

Not only was the dog, Bircham, a Springer Spaniel, absolutely lovely and bounding, and tail-wagging, and smiling all the time, but as she talked to Polly and Helen, Marvellous Murray came out with some unexpected pleasantness. Understanding! Kindness!

What it amounted to was this. Not only did she understand that the Dare was difficult to avoid once it had been put into words, but she also had been told that her Scots accent was difficult for some people and she was going to spend a few moments with each class she taught, sort of translating for them the most difficult phrases. Helpful, or what? Not believing her ears, Polly then picked up that Bircham needed to be walked and played with on a Saturday morning while Mrs Murray was shopping, and would she, Polly, be able to help with that occasionally?

Would she just! A Springer spaniel in her garden? Yes, please! Now then, Helen, I dare you to shake your head and turn that down. I'll kill you, I will!

But no! Wonder of wonders, Helen was smiling, nicely, at her as well as at Marvellous Murray and Bircham.

'I don't know how Polly is keeping quiet,' she said. 'It will be a dream come true, won't it? I just don't need to ask. She'll be delighted to help out, and so will I. Polly?'

'Oh, thank you for the chance, Mrs Murray. I'm so looking forward to it. I didn't even think you had a dog, somehow.' Which was putting it mildly.

She had three phone calls that evening. The first from Linda, whose mother had obviously insisted that she should make an attempt to be a bit friendly, because she came on the phone after Linda had spoken;

'Oh dear, Polly, that was a real mess. Are you OK? Something to be learnt from it all, then I guess you have to move on. I'm angry with Linda, as you can imagine. If there's a 'next time' you stand firm and refuse to be drawn in, will you?'

Polly agreed she would and let Linda's mum speak to Helen. The second call, from Bethany, was all apologies, and an invitation to a sleepover. So that was OK.

The third was - yes, Tom.

'I feel a total fool, Polly,' came after embarrassed greetings.

'You're not a fool,' was the best she could muster.

'I should have stopped you – I should have stopped them and I'm really sorry. It was feeble. Are you OK?'

Polly quickly told him about Mrs Murray's visit and about the Saturday morning arrangement to look after Bircham. 'She was much nicer than I thought, and Bircham's great. I'm so looking forward to helping with him. That's making me feel better.'

'You've never had a dog, you said. Do you want me to come over and help a bit? Springers can be very bouncy and energetic.' A polite little offer that lifted Polly's spirits still further.

Not that she had the remotest idea of how massive a change it would bring into her life. She had read the phrase 'the future is shrouded in mystery' and had thought how exciting it sounded; it had given her a shiver down her back.

She got the same shiver now.

FELICITY'S FALL

Will Ingrams

The Wood
Beneath the branches the day grows long; weary warmth wanes.
Chilly caresses from evening's shivery fingers, scarcely felt at first
Evade daylight's doomed defences,
Dropping velvet veils over bush and bough.

The season is changing.
Bramble thorns, once elegantly piercing, translucently green
Harden their hearts to dry-cracked cruelty,
Stiffen into skeletal brown briars, cat's-claw sharp and hound's tooth hard,
Parched and pitiless.
Autumn creeps in calmly, irresistible and irrevocable.
The generous fruits of summer shrink and dry,
Lusciousness lost with their colours and soft sweetness.
The cold, crackling circle is closing again.

Within the wood creatures feel unexpected urges to gather and store,
Recalling parsimony and prudence.
Lazy summer luxury is lost to hurried harvest,
Anxious hoarding against hazily recollected hardship.
Questing squirrels sail along thin twigs,
Release curled drying leaves to fall, slow and spinning.
They thicken the rustling quilt, hide summer green beneath shells of brown and yellow.
Mice and voles scurry under, searching and hiding.
Bees have it harder too - further forays, fewer finds;
Flowers fade and the time of rest and reserves approaches.

The Fall
Into this circle of Autumn she falls, limbs flailing.
A tiny girl, no taller than a daisy, delicate as a dandelion clock.
Black hair billows, skirts swirl and fingers fail to find anything firm.
Tumbling down, disoriented, falling fast and full of fear.

How has it come to this?
Followed foolish fantasy a step too far, Felicity, she thinks,
And this is now intractably tricky.
A petticoat parachute can't save me,
Its starchy stiffness slows me only slightly.
The woodland floor rushes up, what can a falling girl do?

Bees, Felicity! Seize the bees!
They bumble busily below - she can call to them, surely?
She knows their tone, the essence of bumbleness,
A ringing resonance held in her head,
That flutter of filmy wings that can carry, improbably,
The heft of a huge hairy body with poise and precision.
Focus Felicity! Bond with the bees,
Beam the brain buzz down to the bobbing bumblers.
Help me, my friends, her head hums.
No response, no rescue? Hum harder, hum heavier!

Then...
A quiet quiver begins below,
A hovering hiccup from her nearest neighbour.
The bee tilts up, perceives her plummeting,
Tumbling towards.
Bee brains react rapidly to risk.
Response required! Alert another,
Desperate deployment, bee brother!
Dance into danger with me, fly we fast!

Dropping down, angling in with matched manoeuvres
The bee brothers position precisely as they fall with Felicity.
She smiles, sees arrays of her reflected face in black clustered domes;
Feels friendship and fortitude.
Bee legs extend, come closer to outstretched arms and grasp,
Slippery slick, but firm as they clasp and cling.
Only feet from fracture, Felicity's bees fight the fall,
Begin to buzz, deny descent
Stretching her skyward at last.
Her hair settles softly back, fringing Felicity's face
As the bees hoist her helpfully onto a beech tree limb,
Grey and grippy underfoot as they set her down.

Don't go, brother bees! Felicity pleads.
You arrested me handily, preserved my life when I was lost.

Bounty behoved, brave bumblers!
Bees are bereft of speech
But Felicity's words resonate between their oval eyes,
And a buzzing beams their brainwaves back.
Lost life leaves all lower. Less harm from a little lift, loquacious loner.
They haver a hasty head-dip and wander away, hedge high,
A final hunt before heading homeward.

Felicity flings farewells, then sighs,
Sits to assess her situation.
The beech branch is at moderate height,
But feels far from the floor to tiny Felicity.
Perversely, she ponders,
Its position puts me vertically very far from my city in the clouds.
And how might I master a millimeter of my colossal climb
In clothes chosen to impress princes at parties
And promote paternal pride?

Minutes before but a mile above, Felicity's footfalls
Led her lightly toward a sensitive sister's reception, engagement arranged.
Delicately descending to cloud-ground, Felicity snatched sight of streaking flight,
Soaring shapes of sleekness
Shooting through cloud drifts, twisting and jinking above her head.
The martins flew fast and Felicity followed forward
Entranced by their energy, speed and freedom.
Cloud people take peculiar pride in surface awareness,
An innate understanding of edges and voids.
Their cities and castles hide in close clouds
Floating over the fearsome fauna of Earth
In a time before bigger folk's tyranny triumphs.
Many millenia prior to ploughshares, petroleum and the popular press
Distracted Felicity just stepped too far, and the cloud let her fall.

Timidity is not Felicity's failing.
She swiftly sheds her silky skirt and party petticoats
Leaving her coolly clad in tights and top, ready to trek.
Along the broad bough towards the trunk she trips, keen to climb.
The bole is huge and not so smooth to Felicity's tiny fingers,
Wrinkles and cracks scar the grey gritty beech bark;
Her own bough's branching has waved whorls of wrinkles into the trunk.
She can quickly climb to twice her height
And reach to a bark crack to hoist herself higher.

But then where, Felicity?
These tree trunk traits, welcome whorls and gaps,
Are too far scattered, too rarely erupting.
Felicity gazes up at the vast curved wall and spots the grips she needs,
The hand-holds and foot-cracks,
But all are beyond the keen reach of her little limbs.
She is stuck.

The fact stabs at her bubble of bright buoyancy,
And her mood sags to sombre sense.
Foolish Felicity.
The day is dimming and cold is creeping in.
Night is nigh.
You are lost, alone and far from home,
Spread on this tree
Like a starfish on rock
Arms aching, fingers fit to quit their grip.
Lost indeed.
Fallen.

The Nest
Bumbling back through woodland gloom the bee brothers,
Still tenuously tuned to Felicity's frequencies,
Sense ripples of her desperation waves.
They turn together, and as both bob back to the broad beech
Felicity faintly feels a brain bond and hazards a hope of repeat rescue.
From dusk and dropping dew the bees emerge,
Once more to grasp the grateful girl.
She gushes gratitude and again her heroes hardly hear her thanks.

Plucked and carried courteously,
Felicity wonders where this fortunate flight will finish.
Beneath barely-seen branches,
Between yellowing leaves and shrubs shrinking into shadow
The trio hovers on, heading northwards and down
Through troughs of dank earth odours.
Felicity feels the beat of more bees, a building buzz of converging cousins
And knows their nest is near.
Behind glossy barbs and bloodbright berries of Butcher's Broom bushes
They bear her along to a hole in the brown soil bank.

Set gently down and standing safe
She sees homecoming bees commune and consult.
Agreement reached, Felicity's brother bees busy her along,
Fending her footsteps up to their earthy entrance.
She bends below a canopy, creeping into warm humming closeness,
Urgently alive, active, in a deeper, sweetly dense darkness.
Three dozen bumblers crawl and dance
Around wax nectar pots and close-stacked coddling cells.
As her eyes grow true she can see some are void,
Exhausted of larvae this late in the year.

Her helpful hosts lead her off to one side
Where with care they prepare her a rare resting space
Nibbling nubs of soft cells to a narrow nest nook.
Overwhelmed by their kindness, Felicity smiles
And beams bee vibrations of thanks and surprise.
But attention has lapsed and they wander away
Off to low-buzzing slumber and murmuring rest.
Felicity finds her heart feeling light as her limbs grow heavy
And she lays herself long in the newly-made space
Next to soft sleeping bees.
She begins to reflect on the day's strange events
But too soon she subsides into sweet-breathing rest.

The Dawn
A thin misty presence too dark to call daylight
Arrives at the entrance, a dim dream of dawn.
Too slight to detect as it silently slips
Between soft furry murmurs, through wax wall and wing,
This erosion of night reveals nothing but notions
Of creatures, of life.
Yet they stir, as thin patches of paleness insinuate in
To show slight shapes of bumblers
Suggestions of strength.
Vital vibrations creep deep through the nest,
Quivering to consciousness, starting to stir.

In her special soft space the girl opens her eyes
Surprised by her strange awakening location.
She stretches her shoulders and flexes her neck
Finding four coal-dark eye clusters watching her wake.
She is not apprehensive, but happy her helpers are here.

Bee brainwaves buzz and she hacks tattered scraps about fresh forest forage.
Food images propagate rumbles of hunger - Felicity has eaten nothing for hours.
So she mimes mastication and feeds herself handfuls of edible air
Hoping to broker breakfast.
Other bees in the nest make muscular motions
Boost night-stiffened bodies, warm wings for first flight.
Their fodder is found in the meadows and hedgerows,
Picked piecemeal wherever pale petals persist.
But a plan is prepared for the famished Felicity.

The bigger bee bends to the base of a still-sealed store pot,
Nibbles away at its smooth wall of wax.
When he backs up abruptly, a slow leak has started
A trickle of nectar for her delectation.
A fingerful carries rich scents of the garden,
A bouquet of freesia and rose in her mouth.
There is sweetness supplied here but also refreshment
A lightness of liquid she longed for, unknowing.

Felicity drinks.
Her hands drop delicious dribbles over her tongue.
She keeps on collecting and lapping the liquid
None must be lost to flow down to the floor.

The Departure
Her bees seem pleased with her greedy feeding
And seal the leak neatly when she is replete.
They do not eat with her, preferring their provender wild-provided.
Lighter at last, the nest grows less encumbered,
Most bees have departed to forage for food.
Felicity's bees leave reluctantly too,
The day's duties call and their guest has been fed.

Felicity sits and begins to consider.
The empty earth nest is not wholly unpleasant,
But the silence unsettles, she must make a move.
Unexpressed actions lie coiled in her muscles
Anxious and itching to twist their way out.
The bees have been brilliant, but how could they help now?

They can't hoist her high to her home in the clouds,
Perhaps she could climb just a part of the way?

Stepping softly, and picking a path to the portal,
Felicity follows her departed pals.
Bright, clear sunlight kisses the treetop twigs,
But it angles away beyond the bees' bank
Leaving low shadowed layers of light morning mist,
Mysterious moisture in chill early air.
Head upwards Felicity! A clambering climb warms both body and being.

The Danger
Tackling tussocks and thistles, turning through tangles,
Felicity struggles up to the turf top.
She can now gaze down onto leaf-shedding shrubs
Standing guard at the gates of the autumn wood.
Way off to the west the waving grass plain
Shows her vast shifting shadows of heavenly cloudlands.

A clean breeze keeps the climber cool, but
A slight suggestion of smoke swirls past,
Just a whiff on the wind, forgettable at first.
Yet it bounds back billowing, grows grey and granular,
Drifting and threatening, acrid, alarming.
Becomes bold brewing smoke, much thicker and choking;
Pokes eyes unprovoked, invades nostril and throat.
Fire, Felicity! Dark unknown danger!

Alive on the wind rush the heat and the flames,
Coaxing grass and dry briars to smoulder, to light,
Co-opting them into a cannibal campaign.
Bright blazing brands kindle dry lifeless leaves
And they catch, flare and fly in grotesque resurrection;
Scorched skeletons sail along, dancing and dangerous,
Deliver destruction from thicket to thorn.

Turning tight in alarm Felicity stumbles.
She slips down the recently struggled-up slope,
Rolls and bumps past the nest nook, tumbled and crumpled.
Landing hard, bruised and battered, she lies looking up.
She sees desperate creatures all fleeing the fire,
Running, riding the warm wind, wide-eyed and wild.

Fierce flame-heat above warms Felicity's face,
But her stumbling somersaults seem to have saved her.

The bees must evacuate too.
Summoned by smoke they salvage sweet nectar,
Grow heavy and drowsy, blundering, slow.

The Climb
An alert and familiar bee now finds Felicity,
Trying to help her, to tug her away;
Leads her east between trees till they come to a clearing
A wide space encircling a huge ancient oak.

Felicity's guardian communicates climbing,
Paints patchy pictures, presents possibilities;
Thin twigs in treetops and wings in the wind.
She sees swoop and soar, sunbeam and side-slip,
A sketchy ascent, a cloudward climb.
This mind-misted tale hints at how to head homeward
Rising triumphant to regain her castle.

The story bewitches, but how can she bring this romance to reality?
Listen Felicity, her bee buzzes urgently, climb to the tree top, sail into the sky.

A root finger grips the oak-sheltered ground here,
She treads its tough top skipping lightly and eagerly
Watched and approved by her whisk-winged companion.

She reaches the richly-ridged trunk,
Delves deep in the oak's grey grooves, finding edges for fingers and feet.
With care she can climb in these coarse corrugations,
The chunky oak chimneys that almost enclose her.

At first it goes fast, stretching, hauling and flexing,
The girl gains height steadily, hand over hand.
Then Felicity inches into an impasse,
A dead-ended tunnel between rival ridges.
Yet tight-tucked and stalled she receives help again.
Her benevolent bee still hovers above her
Holding out feet for Felicity's fingertips.

She grips, and he bears her,
Just dropping a little 'til wings flurry faster
To haul her up higher and reach a new runnel;
The girl is then able to climb on and upward.
This feat is repeated whenever she falters,
He lifts her past branches and breaks in the bole.

Shrubs seem small and thin firesmoke drifts by below
From the smouldering black char left after the flames.
Still she reaches and stretches, works her way upwards
The grey oak bark grooves guide Felicity forward.

The trunk divides finally, boughs thin and twisted,
High in the crown of this old mighty tree.
Only thin wind-waved twigs can extend her ascent now.

She has never seen bees bumble this high before,
But he hovers the heavens, tracks breeze-blown meanders
Sends her image impressions of falling, of flight.
Can she conquer her fears, turn her terror to trust,
Leap out from the oak and let fresh fortune find her?

The Flight
From beneath the last leaves her bee's brother emerges;
Could they catch her again if the fantasy fails?
So Felicity gasps and leaps, twig-tossed and tumbling,
Deliciously terrified, arcs through thin air.

She falls fast but not far, for beneath her a dark shape arises,
Blue-black and broad-backed it cushions the girl.
She is suddenly sitting on sleek shiny feathers,
Her fingers feel firm quills to cling to, to grip.
She is safe, saved and soaring, the earth wheels below her.

The second bee brought her this sky-skimming schooner,
Heavenly help to ride higher, head homeward.
Her house martin chariot chirps long and liquid,
Dancing delight in his sky-skimming skill.
His wings work them higher to hang in a thermal
That carries them up into clear higher air.
White rump flashing, he heads for her cumulus cloudland.

Felicity's spirits soar up like the martin
Singing excitement in unfettered flight.
She delights in the height, feels release in the breeze
As misty cloud fringes envelope them gently.
She nudges his neck as she guides the bold bird
Deep into dense drifting vapour.

The cloud castle courtyard awaits her ahead
And homecoming worries arise in her mind.
Will my absence have ruined the royal reception?
My sister is sure to have suffered and swooned.
Will frail father's fears for me now turn to anger?
Should I slip home in silence to see how things seem?

Her bird cannot halt here, Felicity knows,
So she slips herself sideways
To drop as he swoops
Past the first shelf of cloud-ground.
She strokes his sleek neck, as he tilts to release her,
And hopes she communicates copious thanks.
Wings wheel off west as Felicity lands
And looks to locate herself, happily home.

But here, as she turns, comes a party to greet her
An onrushing gaggle of guards, girls and consorts
And following fleetly, her right royal father,
Not angry but beaming,
His arms wide in greeting.

So foolish but fortunate, Felicity feels.

DIPTYCH, ON AND OFF THE WALL

Judith Osborne

The glass reflects a fixed ferocious scowl.
Not because a scowl is what he sought.
No, sir!
But that is what's presented to reflect.
That's the job. That's the remit.
Always has been, always will be.

How many pairs of eyes,
How many fashions,
Over how many decades?
How many faces presented or captured unawares?
Moving shadows of actions in
slices of dim forgotten rooms.
A duel in seventeen something.
Cut and thrust. Elegant violence.

The flashing blades, the buckled shoes, the bar of sunlight –
all chasing each other across and across the then astonished glass.
Now caught, preserved somewhere in the greying, cracking silver
behind the glass.

Genetic deafness makes all scenes mime. Japanese iemoto.
Back then movements wavered jerkily in the smoky candlelight
once the sun was abed.
Even the weeping female beauty, unrecognised, unrecognisable.

Beauty – now more of that would indeed be welcome.
In 1800 were there not masked faces aglitter on occasion?
Well-charged wine goblets held aloft.
Sparkling, swirling fabrics
and many a time a truly beautiful, but sorrowful young lady, dabbing tears
from big brown eyes with a lace kerchief.
She who brought
the tiny child held up to recognise itself and smile –

that was better. That was what he wanted to reflect.
New life. Pleasure. Beaming smiles.

1900 was certainly the worst.
Face to the wall in a dark, dark spider place.
Nothing to see. Nothing to reflect.
An absence and a dying.

Finally a friendly pair of hands gripped the dusty, cobwebbed frame,
administered a wash and brush up, a touch up of silver gilt,
a satisfied smile to throw back.
Ready for more work.

Gone up in the world again, though.
Hanging, it seemed, at the top of a flight of stairs,
eying and weighing up the climbing talking heads
appearing on the topmost step,
only to move right or left and disappear,
presenting little information for the glass to offer back.
Dignified boredom; quiet contemplation the order of the day.

Until that day in the year of Our Lord 2000 when an alarming face – heavy browed, of glittering eye, runny nose and wet shiny lips,
"Millenium move, mate. Move over my beauty and come with me."

Since then just ugly, ugly, ugly.
Who wants to be kidnapped from the ancestral home
to work for a computer hacker of ill repute?

***

Looking into mirrors had never been a voluntarily absorbing pastime for Elizabeth.

Oh, of course there had been the endless preparations for public events in the early years; then she had taken some interest, and even reached a point of experiencing some pleasure in the end product of the makeup and the hair styling. But that was all 50 years go. Half a lifetime ago. Half a century ago.

Now she was involved in the process her mother had referred to in private with such dislike in her own later life – 'fighting a rearguard action against time'.

Yes, well, sneaky splatterings of rain were falling, along with a raucous gale blowing – a real hair-spoiler if insufficient precautions were taken. Thank goodness for the extra hold spray. Plus it would be flesh-chilling; thank goodness for the thermal vest.

Elizabeth actually wished she wasn't past caring about the impact she made in gatherings. There'd always been a layer of excitement. Now that layer was too frequently replaced by stirrings of embarrassment about the family, in the past and present, and into the future.

What indeed was there in the future substantial enough to be worth acknowledging? Only the grandchildren; grandchildren always held some hope – providing they didn't walk round with phones and iPads in their hands constantly so they never read a book properly or spoke to one face to face. Her own had great potential; they were alert and they were kind.

Suddenly Mark Twain's observation popped into her head, "The language of kindness is one that can be heard by the deaf and seen by the blind".

That moved her, energised her for a few moments, so her gaze focussed on the task in hand – it just had to be done, it was a duty like everything else in this Alice-through-the-looking-glass life of hers.

A distant 'How are you going?' the usual code from her husband for 'I'm going to start hassling you about the time.' Made her shuffle on her chair, and frown slightly.

'Five more minutes,' she murmured, then more loudly to reach the adjacent room she responded with <u>her</u> usual code, 'I am fine,' to indicate, 'Just for once leave me alone to get on,' without faith in the outcome.

But that husband had been her rock; after God, the most important rock ever.

'Philip, I'm ready.'

Out of the double doors and into the thousands of flashing cameras and the roaring crowds.

Thank Heaven not that awful Anthem today.

THE TEAPOT

Anne F. Clarke

'Look Matt, look what I've found!' said Jess, her straight brown hair festooned with creeper and moss.

Matt came round the gable end of the old thatched house. It had once been painted in Suffolk pink but was now streaked with green from the chestnut trees towering beside it. He saw his young wife standing in the middle of a bramble bush holding something in her hand.

'I found it on the window sill up there. It's not broken or anything. Just dirty.' Jess handed him a large blue teapot covered in grime and cobwebs.

Matthew stood absolutely still, staring at her treasure, the shock of remembrance chilling his mind and body. 'It's her's Jess. It's Edith's special tea pot.'

Jess scrambled back through the thorny bushes and stood beside him.

'Who is Edith and how do you know this is her teapot?' she said looking up at his ruddy cheeked, bony face.

'Edith and Tom used to farm here, you know, when we bought it The Executors of the late Mr and Mrs Thomas Candler typed on the conveyance. I used to cycle over here when I was a boy. My uncle farmed at the Home Farm across the Common and I had to pass Chestnut Farm to get to my uncle's house. Edith used to save me the conkers off that big chestnut tree at the front. Then she would invite me into the sitting room. I'd tell her about school that week and she'd bring in the tea tray. It was always set with cups and saucers, a plate of newly baked currant shortcakes with butter oozing from the rich sugary pastry and proper leaf tea made in the big blue teapot. This teapot Jess, this lovely old teapot.'

As Matt stood there in the overgrown garden holding the teapot, his childhood memories enveloped him. He always came to see Edith at the end of the summer holidays and helped her pick plums and apples from the old orchard at the end of the garden. The fruit from the Victoria plum tree was fragrant and delicious. He remembered biting into the firm yellow pink flesh, with the juice running down his chin.

He smiled as he remembered the wasps that used to compete with him for the ripest plums. The days were always golden then. He supposed it must have rained sometimes but he couldn't remember. The busy days spent gathering the harvest from his uncle's fields and Edith's garden remained amongst his happiest memories.

'You know Jess, those chestnuts made the best conkers. Everyone at school envied me. I beat everyone in the playground playing conkers. Even the bigger boys used to suck up to me so that I'd give them one. I was really popular for at least a month! Edith used to give me some to take home to Mother as well. She put them in the linen cupboard to keep the spiders away.'

'Where did Edith get the teapot from, Matt?' asked Jess, her face alight with curiosity.

'Well, Jess she loved that teapot and but it did cause a bit of trouble between her and Tom.' Matt laughed. 'I remember one windy October afternoon I had gone to collect the conkers and I asked her about the teapot. She told me how she had bought it during the War when the Americans were stationed on the airfield down the road. She had cycled into Harleston one afternoon and seen it in the ironmongers shop. The glaze on it was the most beautiful blue. She said it made her think of a midsummer sky. She had gone into the ironmongers for candles, a new skimmer for the milk pans and wicks for the paraffin lamps, not a new teapot. In fact she said she didn't need a new teapot. She still used the old cream ironstone one from Tom's mother but she just longed for something bright and cheerful to have in her kitchen.

The long dreary winter days of war depressed her and Tom's meanness made her sad. It came between them, his meanness, she said. She told me she was generous like her father. She wished Tom were more like her father. Her father would have told her to buy the teapot. She told me that she just stood there in the shop until her desire for the teapot became overwhelming and she bought it. She looked me straight in the eye and told me it cost 5s 6d and what did I think of that!'

'Oh dear.' said Jess. 'What did Tom say?'

'Apparently, Tom was furious when she showed it to him and they quarrelled. He shouted at her and asked her what was she doing wasting money during wartime but she said she didn't care. She did say that it was big enough for when the American airmen came for tea. They all admired it and said it lit up the sitting room.'

'Were the Americans stationed here then?' asked Jess.

Matt nodded 'Yes on the airfield at the end of the road. Edith told me that Tom liked the young airmen. He admired their courage and stoicism as they flew raid after daylight raid. They were generous too and Tom always found time to speak to them when he was getting the cows in or cutting the hay on the pasture near the house. They came to tea on Sunday afternoons and to Edith's delight they brought tinned peaches, tinned salmon and bourbon whisky. Tom told Edith once that he imagined that a boy of his would be just like them, sitting drinking tea in front of the fire.'

'Didn't Edith and Tom have any children, then?' said Jess.

'No.' said Matt. 'I think it was a sadness to both of them. Edith made me laugh though, she said that Tom asked her why she couldn't use his mother's teapot. It was a good teapot even though the spout was chipped and the lid had a crack across it. He said she had bought the blue one just to defy him. I think she probably did. She was a very independent woman.'

'What happened to Edith and Tom?' asked Jess.

'The war ended and there were no more young Americans.' said Matt. 'Tom didn't have much enthusiasm for the farm. He was tired and his eyes bothered him, the doctor said he had something called glaucoma. I think Edith was more patient with him, a bit kinder. She didn't use the teapot much as they had little company and for him it was just a blurred image on the kitchen dresser. Tom died in the Spring after the cows had calved. Edith sold the land except the back field and the stackyard but she stayed in the house. I think she enjoyed the money. You can do things with money she told me one plum gathering day. You can go on the bus to Southwold and have tea on the pier. I helped her sort and wash the plums ready for bottling and she made me tea in the blue teapot.'

'It was my uncle who told me that Edith had died.' Matthew continued. 'She had tripped and fallen over the old stone step to the neathouse and broken her hip. She didn't like the hospital. She wouldn't eat they said. I knew she couldn't bear to be away from the farm where she had lived for so long, away from the orchard and the chestnut tree. That's her bedroom window up there.' he said pointing to the casement window framed by the beautiful old chestnut tree.

Jess could see the tears welling up in Matt's eyes and as she hugged him he told her that he hadn't felt able to go to Edith's funeral with everyone else. He wanted to say goodbye to her on his own. So he had waited until the end of winter, picked a handful of the white and green petalled snowdrops from the stackyard at Chestnut Farm and laid them on the bare brown earth of her grave in the village churchyard.

***

It was some time before Jess and Matt moved to Chestnut Farm. There were bricks to be repointed, beams stripped and walls painted. Harvest had come and gone and the chill wind of October blew across the Common.

Conkers had fallen from the big chestnut tree. The day after they moved in Matt went outside to collect some to put in the wardrobes. Edith always told him that it put off the spiders. The teapot, now thoroughly washed, sparkled with cleanliness in the new kitchen which had been installed, complete with brand new Aga. Jess poured boiling water onto the tea leaves in the big blue teapot that stood on the long kitchen table.

Matt, standing in front of the dresser adorned with the new china, asked 'Mugs or tea cups?' Jess smiled gently at him 'Definitely tea cups!'

THE MUSINGS OF HERBERT PREW

D. Green

I suppose you could say it was the Vicar's fault that war was declared in Tombsbury on account he got took by the Lord, or the Devil, one summer's evening. Right quick it was, and he even had a look of surprise on his features after his heart stopped. Or perhaps it was because he never got to finish his favourite tipple of malt whiskey, still filled to the brim in his glass, with his hand outstretched to grasp it.

Due to Vicar Peabody's passing, the Church in its wisdom sent us Vicar Dimball. A personable enough gentleman we thought, until he opened his mouth to emit a whine that grated through your bones reminiscent of chalk on a dry blackboard. He liked to hear the sound of his own voice and a two hour sermon could easily become three, rising and lowering in unison with Bert Hedges' snoring, second pew from the back.

The voice, we the congregation, could have suffered in silence, but Dim by name and dim by nature, he decided to interfere where angels trod softly - our graveyard. Not just any graveyard you understand, but unique. And I, Herbert Prew, starting from the bottom as a lowly grave marker like my father before me and his father before that, holds the august position of Speaker of the Parish Gravediggers United, and Holder of the Visitors Book.

The Parish's pride and joy, the winner of countless awards for presentation; best wild flower display, best nature reserve, rare butterfly display, well kept picnic area, and atmospheric healing qualities. You need to understand that Tombsbury's acres of pride and joy are old, not just old, but ancient dark ages old, and therefore not strictly in the Christian sense.

I remember it was a glorious day, with the sun making its entrance into the world with a sleepy smile. I stood back and admired the shiny new paint on the park benches. Each perfectly located either side of the smart black gateway leading into Tombury's Resting Place of Excellence. Those golden words set on the gilded plaque amidst elegant scroll work, could dazzle the eyesight on a sunny day. Vicar Dimball arrived clad in flowing robes complete with a dog collar so highly starched, he could barely move his head.

I smiled and greeted him with a cheery, 'Good morning.'

The vicar gave me a sharp nod and rubbed his hands together. 'Right Prew, let's get on with it. I want a full inspection of every foot.'

I winced at the grating whine. 'Oh call me Herb, Vicar, everyone does.'

'I disagree with familiarity with staff, Prew. Surnames will suffice and I expect to be addressed as Sir or Vicar, which is my due.'

I mumbled something, can't remember what. All the time thinking oh my, our vicar needs to unbend a little. He needs a pint down at the Druid's Arms and a dance round the maypole to bring a smile to his face. Nothing the old vicar liked better than a jig with the village lasses.

I eyed the vicar's long skirts. 'You might like to borrow some wellingtons, Vicar. It rained last night and the grass in places is long on account of the Rainbow Blue being spotted.'

The vicar gave an exasperated sigh. 'What Prew, is a 'Rainbow Blue'?'

'A rare butterfly, Vicar. The Butterfly Enthusiasts Club will be pouring in here at the weekend hoping to a catch a glimpse. It flies this way every year.'

The vicar thrust out his narrow chest. 'A pack of sightseers traipsing through the graveyard won't do Prew. Won't do at all.'

'With respect Vicar, they don't traipse. They are guided by myself and Bert ...errr...Smithers that is. Vicar Peabody had an agreement with the Club. They get viewing rights and in return the Club paid for a new roof on the church. A signed agreement, Vicar. I can bring it up to the Rectory if you would like to see it?'

Vicar Dimball sucked on his two long front teeth and shifted from one foot to the other. 'Oh, very well, but shoo it away if its still here in two weeks.' He shook out his skirts. 'On with it Prew.'

Aghast, I thought of all the lost revenue through the summer, the excellent cream teas Mrs Teeby provided, the homemade ices the local lasses took such pride in, all those local crafts and knitted gifts the old ladies at Sally's Nearly There Home of Rest, had worked hard at all winter. All those tips that went into the fund for a new greenhouse. The ladies did so like to take an orchid away.

I opened the wrought iron gate and ushered the vicar through to a small crossroads resolutely marching straight ahead not daring to look towards the left.

'What's down there Prew?'

Just a small lie I thought. 'Oh that leads down to the Armitage Meadow, we shall come to that later.' How could I take him into the village's very own pride and joy, the Druid's Dell, complete with resident Druid ghost.

Within the Dell, branches of blossom competed all year round for the best display of colour in every shade of pink and white, cascading their wedding confetti petals across the grass and into the winding brook beyond. No one thought to mention the strangeness of heavy blossoms in thick frost and snow, it was just a fact.

'This bower is known as 'Lover's Corner' and has the best display of fragrant lilacs and bluebell for miles around.'

'It's a graveyard Prew, not a flower show and why is that marble casket lying above ground?' There was a distinct scowl on the vicar's narrow forehead.

'A last request, Vicar. Granny Harris, we laid her to rest ten years back, or rather we set here down here. She wanted the sun's rays to warm her old bones on the days it is out.'

'She's dead Prew, not on holiday.'

'Well the fact is vicar, the village thought a whole lot of Granny Harris. She was a dab hand with a potion, and it's a known fact that white marble is better than silk sheets. Many a village youngster has come into being courtesy of Granny Harris, after a night or two on top of that marble slab. If you take my meaning Vicar.' I decided a smile or wink was not in order as I registered the dark glower on the vicar's face.

His mouth opened and shut twice before he squawked, 'Fornication Prew, in a graveyard. It's heresy.'

I sighed. 'It's called baby-making, Vicar.'

A notebook and pencil were drawn from a deep pocket and the vicar hastily started to make notes. 'Lead on Prew.'

I led the vicar through acres of plots all neatly sectioned off by Yew and Bayleaf hedges. Walked him around the array of Hydrangea bushes that the Chairman of Kew Gardens had been in raptures over. Not a flicker of interest crossed the vicar's face. His only comment, 'You could get ten more plots in here without those bushes.'

'We call this acreage 'Manor's Majestic'.' I waved my hand at the vibrant display of wild flowers. "A botanist's dream, I'm told,' then hastily added, 'Not that we have many visits. The folk up at the Manor at the end of the village have been laid to rest here for centuries. All the servants too, including those three unfortunate housemaids. Back in the 1600's it was, Vicar.

Daisy, Tilly and Mabel were their names. The story goes the then lord and lady were away from home and their drunken nephew and his friends, chased those poor girls through the Manor until, in terror of rape and murder, they jumped from an attic window to their deaths on the flagstone courtyard below. The nephew mysteriously died, something he ate. His name has been expunged from the village records and no one knows where he is buried.'

I took a step back. 'Are you all right Vicar, you're looking a bit white.'

'Suicides. There are suicides in my graveyard?'

'Not in the least Vicar. Three unlawful killings surely?'

The vicar waved his hand and wrote furiously in his notebook. 'What else is this unnatural village harbouring. What's over there?'

My gaze followed the vicar's pointing finger and I gulped.

Far beyond the stream lay the splendid 'Old Gods' Maze', three acres of flowering hedges, where offerings to the Old Gods festoon the branches of the mighty Oak tree at its centre; the shady foliage making the perfect setting for a picnic area in the heat of summer.

'Just a picnic area, Vicar.'

'Picnic area?,' he thundered.

I winced at those shouted words.

'You'll be telling me next a witch sells ice cream to visitors in the summer months, and the village has ghosts.'

How right he was, I thought.

Vicar Dimball drew himself upright, his skirts wet to his knees. Pencil poised. 'Right Prew, this is what you and your henchmen will be doing as of tomorrow.'

To this day I remember the cold slide of dread through my vitals, the feather-like tendrils of ice along my spine, as I hastily glanced around expecting a spectre of wrath to rise up from the grassy dell where butterflies frittered.

Later, I repeated word for word to a stunned audience in the Druid's Arms what Vicar Dimball intended.

'Modernisation he called it. Wants gravel paths, the grass mowed regularly, park benches and neat plaques on every grave, and the Hydrangeas ripped out to make room for ten future occupants.'

'What about Armitage Meadow?' Bert picked his pint up from the bar and took a gulp.

I pictured Armitage meadow and all we hoped to achieve there. I couldn't wait to get my spade into the rich new earth and I wasn't alone. I had seen Harold my second in command, covertly eyeing up old Mrs Farrell, practically rubbing his hands together, so fragile was her health.

'I dare not take him there. He'd probably want to build on it.'

'Sacrilege,' old Horace had declared. 'Wanton destruction of our village heritage.'

All those gathered nodded in agreement.

I turned to Gladys the barmaid. 'Oh best get word to Reggie that the Mystery Tours are cancelled for the time being.'

There was a chorus of groans.

'What did he say about the Druid's Dell and the Maze?' asked Mavis, the baker's wife.

'I didn't dare show him. I thought he would have an apoplexy.' I took a sip of our homemade brew, Lightning Strikes. Two pints could give the uninitiated a fair wobble, three the floor moved and four, well you could be away with the fairies in no time.

'I told him, Tombsbury's graveyard was revered and no one had the right to change it. Ungodly he call it. Trouble, just like I was, he told me.'

'What are we going to do?' asked Harold.

I made a decision then. 'Right lads, I hereby call a strike.'

A picket line was drawn at the church with only the Vicar allowed in. Every evening a copy petition was tacked to the church entrance and torn down again by the vicar the following morning. Fortunately no new graves were required.

Not one villager crossed the church threshold and Mrs Teeby, the owner of the local tea rooms, went around with a permanent smile affixed, standing room only during bible readings.

Stalemate was declared.

Over the next three weeks, Gravediggers United, pondered long into their after hours ale tankards.

'There are some fine toadstools up in the woods,' Bert had commented.

'That loose plank on the stairs up into the belfry could get looser, he is always up and down there playing with his bells,' Alf suggested.

Gloomily, I stared into my tankard. One more week and the digger would be here.

'Well lads, Plan A – negotiation was pointless, Plan B – our strike has achieved nothing except get me the sack.' I looked up from my pint. 'Got the letter this morning in his own fair hand.'

'But he can't do that,' exclaimed Chesterfield our oldest resident, and as sharp as a tack. 'States clearly in the Parish Records offspring of the Prews, Smithers and Lockes are the ones to tend the graveyard unless there are no offspring.'

He raised an eyebrow. 'With Herb's three, Bert's two and Harold's five we won't be running out of offspring for many a year. I'll go up and have words with this vicar tomorrow, show him the Records.'

'I appreciate that Chesterfield, but it's not about me. It's the graveyard I'm worried about. I think Plan C is called for. Are we all agreed?'

A resounding 'aye' echoed through the pub.

I may not have mentioned Mrs Oddby, the vicarage housekeeper. One of six daughters of a daughter of Granny Harris, and our resident white witch or black, depending on what the occasion called for. Alone she was formidable and all the sisters together, well, better than your own army.

'Oh, no bother Mr P,' Mrs Oddby informed me with a smile and a wicked gleam in her green eyes. 'Sir B will sort him out in no time.'

Music to my ears those words were.

'Don't you fret. Put that smile back on your face. Druid Peter is a particular friend of Sir B, and he won't take kindly to interlopers trying to change matters. He's just come back from the bakers for me and is having his porridge and honey. I'll drop a word in his ear.'

I had a whimsical image of a grocery bag making its stately way along the High Street self-propelled.

I should explain that Sir Basil was one of Tombsbury's oldest ghosts, a badly wounded cavalier from a nearby battlefield, who had been taken in by the villagers and never left.

Do ghosts eat? I made no attempt to go there.

I didn't see Vicar Dimball depart Tombsbury, rather, I heard the screech of tyres and saw the dust cloud he left behind.

'How?' I asked Mrs. Oddby.

'Oh, I arranged for the vicar to view Sir B and old Lord Axel's weekly fencing match.'

'But Lord Axel was beheaded by the Roundheads.'

'Yes, makes for an interesting spectacle. I'll send his belongings back to the Ministry shall I?.'

That evening Gravediggers United raised their tankards in a toast to Sir Basil and Lord Axel, the saviours of Tombsbury and of course, Mrs Oddby.

Vicar Mead, a delightful man, resides with us now. He's a dab hand with the weeding and has been seen chatting with Druid Peter. The Vicar likes nothing better than a picnic beneath the old Oak tree, with the pagan offerings fluttering overhead. Never turned a hair when he was asked to move along the picnic table to make room for Daisy, Tilly, and Mabel.

Oh, and Sir Basil is in his element, I understand the Vicar plays a wicked game of chess.

All is well in Tombsbury.

SECATEURS AND SABOTEURS

John Antram

'Here comes Jonas with the secateurs,' said Lady Diana to Attleborough Beauty. 'Now we're for the chop.'

'And not before time,' the neighbouring rose bush replied. 'After pruning we'll be getting upsized pots.'

'Yes, let's not talk about being pot-bound again,' said Diana. 'That hybrid up from Essex went on about it yesterday for far too long.'

'She got well pruned this morning. You thought the screams were from the children.'

Across the aisle in the garden centre a group of primulas, sitting in trays, were sniggering. 'We don't need pruning,' they shouted to the roses.

'You woody things need too much care from the humans,' added a lone Lily of the Valley, in its own shiny black pot adjoining their display.

All the plants quieted down to listen, as they usually did when Jonas, the foreman, and Paula his new assistant, came towards them. If any of the garden-centre staff were talking, the plats wanted to hear. It was this way they heard the news, for instance, sudden departures of old friends or batches of novices arriving from distant nurseries.

'Look at that woman coming in, with the giant, yellow handbag. She's from that garden centre at Needham, you know, the one the boss said was importing the diseased ash saplings.' Paula tried hard not to stare but noticed a sour-faced, thin, middle-aged woman glance in their direction before proceeding through to the café.

'She's not a happy bunny. Perhaps she's planning to do some shoplifting.' Paula was thinking it must soon be time for their tea-break. 'Are we going to re-pot these roses after our tea or leave it till tomorrow?'

'First thing in the morning,' said Jonas. 'I'm as dry as a ….as a….very dry thing. Let's stop now.' The two workers disappeared away to their potting shed.

'So, did you hear? We're getting larger pots in the morning. That's something to look forward to. Oh, look Diana; here comes that woman they were talking about. What's she getting out of her bag?'

'Some kind of spray can. Oh no! She's doing something to those primulas.'

The screams from the primulas were shrill and agonised, as some kind of glyphosate soaked into their leaves and began its burning, poisoning process towards the roots.

'She's moving over to the petunias. It'll be us next if Jonas doesn't come back soon!' The noise from the primulas became overwhelming as the petunias joined in. The two roses and the lily saw Jonas and Paula emerge from the potting shed, and watched as Paula hurried up the aisle towards them. She stopped at the primulas, whose groans were gradually becoming moans, gasps and gulps, and looked across at the petunias.

'Hey!' Jonas called, 'We're supposed to be watering the hedgerow plants.'

Paula seemed to ignore him and began bending over the primulas, some of whom were saying, 'It hasn't rained; we've not been watered yet, why are we wet?' Others were groaning, some were shouting.

'Yellow handbag: Spray. Yellow handbag: Spray.'

Paula turned to Jonas. 'Is that woman still here? The one you said was from Needham?'

He looked at her blankly. 'What? Why?'

'Find the boss,' Paula cried, 'that woman's a saboteur. We must catch her before she leaves.'

'How do you know?' said Jonas.

'Check that handbag of hers. These plants have been sprayed with something to kill their roots.'

Later, after the angry woman had been taken away in the police car, the plants settled down for the night. The bedding plants had been thoroughly hosed and were likely to survive their ordeal.

'What a day,' said Lady Diana, 'and what a joyous outcome. It's almost as if Paula can hear us. I felt a definite empathy with her. Some of us will have to watch what we say.'

'Joyous outcome?' said her companion. 'I'd call it disastrous.'

'But don't you realizse, my dear? We've been blessed with Jonas for months. He's certainly got the green fingers which nurture us, but now the management has recruited Paula who will grow the fingers alongside Jonas, but already has the green ears!'

WHO DO YOU THINK YOU ARE?

Joan Roberts

My family tree has become a forest
The line of decent too mixed to decipher
Parents and grandparents an ancestral stew
A melee of cousins from far afield
Are joined through blood, and then like the Swallow
Move each summer, settling nowhere.

The original path from an Ice Age nowhere
Probably to some northern forest
Winter's bite forcing them like the Swallow
South and west on a path yet undeciphered
And leading to open fields
Infusing new blood into the stew

Roman invasion adds meat to the stew
The tribal home thus far is nowhere
Slaves and workers soon flee the field
Forced to return back north to the forest
For reasons they cannot decipher
Reasons those left find hard to swallow

Great floods and disasters and the Swallow
Flies east, some follow; migration diluting the stew
The future cannot be deciphered
For those who have evolved from nowhere
Is their history to be in the forest?
Or will some remain to plough the field?

Pogroms and wars force many to leave the field
To seek other paths than those of the Swallow
They cross the sea away from the forest
A throng of diverse tribes thickening the stew
And others too who have left their nowhere
And speak foreign tongues that cannot be deciphered

The journey continues and they learn to decipher
Parlance and praxis from many fields
Many a somewhere arises from nowhere
Some put down roots others are nomads like the Swallow
Changing the mix swelling or shrinking the stew
As trees die off new shoots maintain the forest

My lineage hard to decipher not a constant like that of the Swallow
Diverse roots from many a far field reinforcing the strength of the stew
Two fledgling shoots of nowhere begets a colossal and varied forest

THE COLONEL AND THE FLY

Joan Roberts

Colonel Tristan Lloyd Hunter-Johns dropped himself drunkenly onto the side of his bed spilling almost a quarter of a glass of brandy down his pajamas. He looked at the clock, it was 2.15. It had been an interesting dinner, not as enjoyable of course as when it was a male only affair, this modern business of bringing along the wives was a rotten idea. Except for that jolly little thing that March had in tow. Shapely little blond, huge affair in front, kept jiggling up and down when he made her laugh; name of Chablis or Champagne; odd idea calling one's daughter after wine; and that little lisp, quite fascinating. He picked up his book, Winston Churchill's The Birth of Britain (A History of English Speaking Peoples) Volume 1. *Damn good writer Churchill, bloody awful soldier of course, but good heavy book, worth reading.* Not that he had read much, it was too large to hold up and he found by the time he had read and re-read a couple of pages he'd had enough; very good for sending him off to sleep though.

Then he heard the buzzing. It was above his head at first, gradually moving around to his left ear. He batted it away, couldn't stand flies. He'd have to get rid of it before he switched the light out and went to sleep. He could just make it out settled on the wall above the side of the family heirloom. This was a heavy set, dark oak console table, with two thick bulbous, highly carved legs; it had been the object of the most recent debacle between him and the lady wife, Marjorie.

'The bedroom is no place for that awful thing,' she had complained again. 'It's far too heavy to move when I'm cleaning and the legs and the feet are difficult to dust with all those lumps and bumps. It's a miserable looking, ugly thing sitting there passing judgment on us in the corner whilst we're sleeping.'

'It has been in my family for generations and I find it comforting. It very much reminds me of my dear departed mother who loved it. If you don't like it then you can sleep in the other bedroom.' Marjorie could appreciate the likeness to his mother only too well which was part of the problem. A heated argument developed and he lost his temper, pulling open the door just as Marjorie was about to leave and catching her in the face with it. Hence the black eye that she was now nursing and the reason she had not accompanied him tonight. In fact Marjorie had gone to bed early but had heard him come home, as she was sure they had in the next village, and locked her door lest he found it necessary as he sometimes did to continue the row.

The fly was on the move again, around and around, up and down, disappearing from view and then buzzing in one ear and then the other. It settled again on the wall opposite so he took Winston's tome and threw it. *Blast! Missed again Winston!* He got up and scrambled under the bed for the copy of the Telegraph he had been reading last night. Rolling it up into a tube he stood by the bed waiting for the fly to give itself away. There it was settled on the wall above the heirloom and he crept forward, paper baton at the ready. Keeping his eye on the fly he did not see Winston on the floor and tripped, falling forward and catching his head fully on the large hard corner of the problematic antique.

***

'He was your father! You cannot under any circumstances not be there at his funeral; it would be such bad form not to attend,' Marjorie pleaded with the children and in the end they had agreed to be there.

The cortege left the house at 09.50 in true military efficiency to reach the small village church by 10.00 hours. The family heirloom left for auction at 10.10. At first it had been Marjorie's intention to chop it up for firewood, but then she thought about its great age and decided to see how much it was worth. Perhaps she might buy a new, small, modern car, something she knew would have really irritated her late husband who would never part with their gas, guzzling, ancient, and in her opinion highly over rated, Jaguar v. something or other.

After the service back at the house many of the guests commented upon the Colonel's bravery and outstanding career. Marjorie stood by the fireplace flanked on both sides by her son Corinthian and her daughter Boadicea both sporting particularly dour expressions, which most of the guests mistook for grief. Myrtle and Daisy, two WVS veterans, who had arranged the flowers in the church and had been serving the tea and sandwiches, just like the old days, looked toward the little group at the fireplace, who were joined by those wishing to take their leave.

'I say what a terrible thing to happen after all the action he had seen?' suggested Lieutenant March. 'Have you met my fiancé Chardonnay?'

Marjorie noted his diminutive partner who had an enormous chest which appeared to have a life of its own under the rather tight bodice she was wearing, and had to stop herself from adjusting her own sensible 'cross-your-heart' bra straps.

'He wath tho funny,' lisped Chardonnay, 'the more I laughed the more funny thingth he found to thay.' Boadicea snorted and took a handkerchief from her sleeve to cover her face. 'Oh I'm tho thorry I didn't mean to upthet you, but he wath thuch a lovely man.'

'Dignified aren't they, their type, stiff upper lip and all that?' said Myrtle.

'I heard he was a bit of a bully,' said Daisy lowering her voice. Myrtle shook her head.

Oh really, I heard Mrs. Hunter-Johns saying to the General that the Colonel couldn't hurt a fly.'

THE YEW TREE

Anne F. Clarke

Hundon St John was a pretty village. The local Estate agents referred to it as nestling in the heart of the Suffolk countryside and offering an idyllic lifestyle that is to those with sufficient money to buy into it. It did not, of course, take into account the lifestyle of the people who had always lived there.

People like Arthur Browning who had moved to the village after the war. His Dad had been the blacksmith in the village of Hundon St Martin next door. Arthur didn't like horses much and being a smithy held no appeal, so he used an inheritance from his Grandad to buy the garage up on the hill. He was good at the work too, and when he married Betty, the school master's daughter, he became a respected member of village society.

Arthur and Betty lived in a cottage down Church Lane. The lane ran past the church towards the allotments and wound its way up the hill to his garage. It was a substantial cottage with a good vegetable garden and orchard. It had black and white windows, two chimneys, a pretty herbaceous border down both sides of the garden path and a yew hedge which separated it from the flint cottage next door. Arthur liked the yew hedge but thought that it lacked substance so he planted a yew tree at the end of the hedge on the boundary of his property with the flint cottage.

The flint cottage belonged to an old lady called Mrs Minchin who had lived there long before Arthur had moved next door. Nobody knew much about her and she had few visitors except for a niece called Miss Minchin. Betty and Mrs Minchin exchanged 'good mornings' over the yew hedge when they hung out the washing. Arthur and Mrs Minchin nodded politely at each other in Church on Sunday mornings when he held the collection plate in readiness for her offering.

Arthur's yew tree grew bigger and stronger, unlike Mrs Minchin who grew older and weaker. Her hair, which was already white and thin, grew sparse and she walked with two sticks instead of one. Then Mrs Minchin died. There was much speculation in the village as to what would happen to the flint cottage. Arthur and Betty speculated too.

Betty said 'It would make a nice home for a family with children. There's plenty of room to play in the garden.'

'It could be someone mad on cars.' said Arthur. 'I could do with another customer.' And then they had a visitor. It was Mrs Minchin's niece. She knocked on the front door. Arthur opened it.

'Morning, Browning.' said Miss Minchin. 'Thought I'd come to see you. I've retired from the city and I'm moving in. Hope that tree's not in the way.' Then she left.

Arthur shut the front door. He just couldn't help it, he took an instant dislike to her. From her blue rinsed hair to her tweed skirt, sensible shoes and effortless air of command, he recoiled. He walked back into the kitchen.

Betty said. 'Would you like a cup of tea, dear?'

'I should think I would.' spluttered Arthur. 'Do you know what she called me?'

'I've no idea,' said Betty, lying through her teeth, as she had heard every word. 'What did she call you?'

'Browning,' said Arthur indignantly. 'Browning! Who does she think I am, her bloomin' gardener?'

'Calm down, dear,' said Betty trying not to giggle. 'Remember your blood pressure. You've gone quite red in the face.'

Arthur drank his tea and awaited the arrival of the removal men. Meanwhile the yew tree flourished and Arthur enjoyed the many compliments he received on its handsome appearance. However, he failed to notice that one branch had begun to lean a little over the garden path next door.

Miss Minchin arrived two weeks later accompanied by a large removal van, one man and his boy. She parked her car in the garage and walked up the path to the lane. The removal men tried to back the van onto the garden path but the yew tree was in the way. She looked at it with dislike.

'Sorry missus,' said Fred the van driver, 'I can't get any closer, 'cos of that branch.'

'Dratted tree.' muttered Miss Minchin frowning. Then she had an idea. 'Won't be a minute, my man.' she called out to Fred as she walked back to the garage.

'What's she doing now?' said the boy George.

'Don't know,' said Fred, 'but if she calls me my man anymore I'll drop her furniture.'

Miss Minchin came back, armed with a large sharp pair of tree secateurs.

'What are you a'goin' to do Missus?' said Fred looking alarmed. 'That branch belongs to your neighbour!'

'Not while it's in my garden, it isn't.' she said. 'It's got to go!'

It was only when he had come back from working in the garage that Arthur saw the removal men unloading Miss Minchin's substantial mahogany furniture. She was outside supervising. Arthur could hear her strident tones over the hedge. Betty came outside.

'I do think it might be neighbourly Arthur if you offered to help,' she whispered 'perhaps they might all like a cup of tea and a piece of cake.'

The thought of Betty's delicious Victoria jam sponge being consumed by the harridan next door nearly choked him but he sallied forth regardless. He walked up the garden beside the hedge and on to the lane when he saw Miss Minchin standing next to the yew branch holding what looked like a pair of bolt croppers. He was horrified. He tried to grab them but it was too late. Miss Minchin's strong fingers brought the blades together either side of the wood. Crack went the offending branch and landed on the path at his feet. He reached down and picked up the now detached bit of his precious tree.

'What have you done, you wicked old woman. My lovely tree. You've murdered it!' he cried in anguish.

Miss Minchin advanced towards him and they eyeballed each other through the spiky leaves.

'It was in my way, Browning. Get used to it.' she shouted in his face.

When the enormity of her crime finally reached his consciousness, Arthur gave the most blood curdling shriek and whacked Miss Minchin over the head with the branch. Miss Minchin, in genuine fear of her life, turned and raced down the path, around the back of the cottage and up by the lane with Arthur in hot pursuit, brandishing his bit of yew. Fred and George hid behind the van.

Betty, alarmed by Miss Minchin's screams raced up the garden, followed Arthur down the path, around the cottage and out on to the lane. She tried to catch up with them but collapsed on the grass outside the allotments quite out of breath. Betty knew Arthur could run fast, however, she could not help but admire Miss Minchin's remarkable turn of speed as she sprinted down the lane towards the churchyard.

Meanwhile, Miss Minchin, in her effort to escape the homicidal, branch waving, lunatic, vaulted over the church gate and ran straight into the Vicar coming back from choir practice. Unfortunately, the village grave digger had been preparing a new grave near the path. He had gone home for his tea and had planned to complete the task that evening. On his return half an hour later, he was totally unprepared for the sight of Miss Minchin embracing the vicar at the bottom of the hole he had just dug.

Arthur arrived at the same moment, still clutching the yew branch, and issuing the most bloodthirsty threats in the direction of his new neighbour. The choir master managed to disarm him whilst the Vicar escorted Miss Minchin back to the Vicarage. The grave digger took Arthur to the pub.

The next morning Arthur woke up with the most terrible headache. Betty was in the process of telling him that a mixture of emotion, exercise and alcohol was a really bad idea when he sat bolt upright in bed and said 'Betty, this is war. I shall defend my yew tree to the bitter end.'

'Arthur Browning,' said Betty in exasperation 'you are a mechanic, not a Free French commando. I should never have given you that book of Winston Churchill's speeches. It's gone to your head.'

Later that week the Vicar, in the interests of Christian charity, made Arthur and Miss Minchin apologise to each other.

'Now Arthur,' said the Vicar, 'I do believe you have something to say to dear Miss Minchin.'

'I'm sorry that I chased you up the lane.' said Arthur, looking anything but sorry.

'Come now, Arthur,' said the Vicar, 'you can do better than that.'

Arthur gritted his teeth and said quickly before he could change his mind. 'I'm really sorry. It won't happen again.'

'And Miss Minchin,' said the Vicar encouragingly, 'have you anything to say to dear Arthur?'

Miss Minchin wiped away an imaginary tear. 'Very sorry, Browning. I won't do it again.'

'Splendid,' said the Vicar beaming at them both 'now shake hands. All is forgiven and forgotten.'

Arthur almost believed in Miss Minchin's tearful remorse. However, when they shook hands and she held his in a vice like grip that almost halted his circulation, he revised his opinion.

'Betty,' he said the day after the handshakes 'I bet she's not sorry. You mark my words she doesn't like my yew tree. What do you think?'

Betty looked at him furiously. 'I think, Arthur Browning that she's about as sorry as you are. Don't annoy her anymore.'

Unfortunately, Arthur did not heed his wife's wise words. He was careless with some broad leaved weed killer and accidentally on purpose dripped it over her primulas. Miss Minchin retaliated by blasting his wall flowers with her pressure washer when she cleaned her car. These minor hostilities continued. However, neither of them had forgotten the yew tree, which remained apparently untouched.

Thus Arthur remained vigilant but Miss Minchin grew vengeful. Only the secret demise of the yew tree would satisfy her.

Every morning before Arthur was up she would saunter down the garden path, whip out the secateurs that she carried in her pocket and snip off miniscule pieces of root and branch. Frustratingly this did not yet appear to have the desired effect. Then Arthur and Betty went on holiday for a week.

The day after they left Miss Minchin was sitting in the garden reading a free gardening magazine when an article caught her eye. It concerned compost. The experts recommended the addition of a certain concentrated solution in order to break down vegetation, particularly root and branch. Miss Minchin smiled.

She rose early the next morning, filled a receptacle that had belonged to her late Aunt, walked up the path to the yew tree, snipped of more roots and poured the solution over what was left. The leaves of the yew tree began to wilt and grow pale. It did not look well. Miss Minchin grew reckless and repeated the process at night.

By the time Arthur and Betty returned, Miss Minchin was almost triumphant. The morning after his return from holiday Arthur woke early and decided to walk round the vegetable garden. As he came round to the front of the cottage he caught a glimpse of Miss Minchin venturing up her garden path in her nightdress. He crept quietly along the hedge until he reached the yew tree. He could not believe his eyes, it was turning yellow. As he stood upright to have a better look he came face to face with Miss Minchin who had obviously been in the process of anointing the tree with the deadly solution.

Arthur was filled with rage. He turned bright red as the blood rushed to his head. He tore down the path, flung open the front door and unlocked the gun cabinet. Then he took out his 12 bore and loaded it with two cartridges. At that moment Betty rushed down the stairs.

'Arthur, Arthur. Whatever's happened?' Betty cried in alarm.

'What's happened, what's happened?' said Arthur still red in the face. 'She's peed on my tree and killed it!'

In his haste to get out of the front door and avoid his wife's effort to grab the shotgun, Arthur tripped over the step and accidentally fired both barrels blasting Miss Minchin's chimney pots to pieces. Miss Minchin, still clutching her Aunt's chamber pot containing the mixture of Jeyes Fluid and early morning pee, feared she had been shot and promptly fainted by the garden gate.

***

Sadly, Miss Minchin appeared to lose interest in country living after that. She put the flint cottage on the market and retired back to London. Arthur was bound over to keep the peace by the magistrate. The Vicar kindly testified to his usual good behaviour so he got off with a small fine. And Betty? Ever practical, she asked the grave digger to cut down the yew tree and save the wood for Arthur's coffin.

THE ANNUAL GARDEN PARTY

Joan Roberts

It was the Annual Garden Party and they were queueing at the door.
It's the main event in these parts, and has been since the war.
Deidre wore her best hat. The weather looked just fine.
Two awnings and a beer tent, and a stall for homemade wine.

Some guests had been excluded: John Ross and Jake McTier,
Mr Dyson, from the Co-op, and that fuss about the beer!
Others though were welcome and were pushing at the gate,
Mrs Newson, from the cleaners, Dilys Thompson and her Kate.

Dan Packman, his new girlfriend, the Nugent's from the florists,
Mary Carver, from Stoat's Farm, Tom Jackson, Rose, and Horace.
Macgrew and Charlie Pugh from 'How Dja Like Ya Shed'
Were invited but declined to see a football match instead.

The guests walked round the garden, which was looking rather grand,
And crowded round the centre, to hear the Village Band.
There was Andrea on squeeze-box and Nikki on the flute
Richard on tin whistle, he's always 'on the toot.'

John tuning the piano, 'One Man Went to Mow,'
Joan late with her violin, she couldn't find the bow.
Dena on the bongos, Mike and Julie on Guitar
Anne and Judith on maracas, sending signals to the bar.

Bill Carver and Stan Newson look forward to this day;
A chew, a brew, and shanty songs to while the time away.
Ben and Susan Tucker from North Virginia Lane
Were looking rather sozzled, they won't be asked again.

The Vicar and Anne Price, danced a hornpipe much too fast,
Caused Joan to drop her fiddle which landed on the grass.
Before she could retrieve it the Vicar tripped and fell,
Knocking Anne Price into John Stokes, Steve Buckman, and George Snell.

The stage began to buckle and the band began to rock,
Mike grabbed a piece of awning and a clump of Julie's frock.
Judith hit a high note as she fell against a chair,
Anne fell into Dena, who threw her bongos in the air.

Ric knocked Nikki into John who fell into some thistle
(Three weeks later and an op. they found the penny whistle.)
Andrea and her squeeze-box fell onto Martin Glenn
(They've been squeezing one another quite a lot since then.)

The awnings both tumbled and the beer-tent sagged and fell
Covering Bill Newson and half the town as well.
Altogether quite a party, and as the light began to fade
An ambulance was called, and the fire brigade.

A tragedy averted, and nobody was hurt
Some dignity was lost; there was some writhing in the dirt.
On his way home from the pub Mr Dyson saw the heap
He took himself to bed and laughed himself to sleep.

For more information about BigSky Writers, please go to this link:
http://bigskywriters.wordpress.com/

Made in the USA
Charleston, SC
14 December 2014